Blitzcat

Robert Westall

MACMILLAN CHILDREN'S BOOKS

First published 1989 by Macmillan Children's Books

This edition published 2002 by Macmillan Children's Books
a division of Macmillan Publishers Limited
20 New Wharf Road, London N1 9RR
Basingstoke and Oxford
www.panmacmillan.com

Associated companies throughout the world

ISBN-13: 978-0-330-39861-9
ISBN-10: 0-330-39861-X

15 17 19 18 16

A CIP catalogue record for this book is available from
the British Library.

Phototypeset by Intype London Ltd
Printed and bound in Great Britain by Mackays of Chatham plc, Kent

Blitzcat

Robert Westall was born in 1929 on Tyneside, where he grew up during the Second World War. He studied Fine Art at Durham University, and Sculpture at the Slade in London, before teaching art in schools in the north of England. He was also a branch director of the Samaritans, a journalist and an antique-dealer. Between 1985 and his death in 1993, he retired to devote himself to his writing.

His first novel for children, *The Machine Gunners*, published by Macmillan in 1975, won the Carnegie Medal. He won it again in 1982 for *The Scarecrows* (the first writer to win the medal twice), the Smarties Prize in 1989 for *Blitzcat*, and the Guardian Award in 1991 for *The Kingdom by the Sea*.

Reviews of Robert Westall's work:

'A writer who managed to combine literary excellence with an immense talent for capturing the imagination and interest of child and, in particular, young adult readers'
Independent

'Westall was a writer of rare talent. We shall miss him, but he has left us such a wonderful legacy'
Michael Morpurgo, *Guardian*

Books by Robert Westall

For Felicity Trotman, who told me about the real Lord Gort, and made this book possible.

Author's Note

Even the most sceptical zoologists now accept that cats can find their way home over several hundred miles, just like carrier-pigeons. But many think that cats have a greater power – psi-trailing.

In America in the late fifties, a Mid-Western vet saved the life of a cat brought in after a road accident, and adopted her. The only after-effect of the accident was that the cat had an enlarged fifth neck-vertebra. Later, moving to the West Coast, the vet left the cat behind with friends.

Several months later, a cat of the same colour and marking dropped in through the window of his West Coast surgery. Incredulous, he felt her neck and found the same enlarged vertebra. The cat had psi-trailed him over 1500 miles.

Professor J. B. Rhine of Duke University has since studied over three hundred cases of alleged psi-trailing, and authenticated more than fifty. That's why you'll find psi-trailing in this book.

Otherwise, it's a mixture of fact and fiction. Anybody with a day-by-day history of the Second World War will find I have moved events around a little. But all the war incidents really did happen.

R.A.W.   May 1988

1

Sergeant Millom got up on the twenty-seventh of May after another sleepless night. Outside his one-man police station, the sun shone on the little river that danced through the village. The clock in the tall tower of Beaminster church chimed eight, disturbing the pigeons on the parapet. A horse and cart passed, its clop and rumble echoing between the honey-coloured houses.

It should have been peaceful, but the warm east wind carried, like persistent distant thunder, the rumble of German guns. Jerry had reached the French Channel Ports. The King of the Belgians had surrendered. The British Expeditionary Force and their commander, Lord Gort, were trapped around Dunkirk with their backs against the sea.

The news on the radio sickened Sergeant Millom. All the tripe about planned strategic withdrawals, and our troops being in high fighting spirits, and how many Jerry tanks the French 75s were knocking out. The newspapers sickened him, too, with photographs of grinning Tommies giving the thumbs-up. Probably photos a month old. They wouldn't be grinning now, poor sods. Even if they weren't lying dead in some Belgian ditch with the rats at them. Sergeant Millom had fought in the trenches in the last lot; he had never managed to forget the rats . . .

Neither could he forget that Jerry was only nineteen miles away, across the Channel, from an England that dreamed defenceless in the morning sun, its only army trapped around Dunkirk. And among that army, his Tom. Tom was all he had left since Agnes died. He kept remembering Tom laughing on his fifth birthday. Teaching Tom to ride his first bike. Tom still laughing when he went to join up and do his bit, though he wasn't any kind of fighter. Tom was a motor-mechanic, with the Service Corps. He hadn't minded Tom going off to France, because he'd be a mechanic, safe miles behind the lines. But now . . . he hadn't heard from Tom for a fortnight. Since the Jerry push started.

Tom and the rats. He could hardly see straight for thinking about Tom and the rats. And suppose Jerry invaded England? Won? What was left to stop him, with the Army trapped around Dunkirk? As a policeman he'd have to work with Jerry, keeping law and order in the village. But working with Jerry would make him a traitor, a Quisling. Unless he refused and resigned. But Jerry might shoot those who refused and resigned. Who'd look after the village then? Some Gestapo swine in jackboots, kicking people around . . .

He was still fretting over his shaving when a knock came at the door. He answered it with the soap on his face. A stranger; nasty-looking bloke in a black trilby hat and long grey overcoat, in spite of the heat. Millom distrusted all strangers now. Jerry had dropped paratroops in Holland and Belgium, disguised as vicars and nuns. So Millom was sharp with him, though he guessed the stranger was another

2

copper, if only from the size of his highly polished boots.

'Hillfield. Inspector. Special Branch.' The man produced his official card, and stared rudely at the soap on Millom's face. 'Don't stand there dithering, Sergeant. We've got a spy to catch.'

Millom gaped. 'Here? In Beaminster?' He knew everybody. Poachers, wife-beaters, drunks. But a *spy*?

'Woman. Name of Wensley. Florence Wensley. Brereton House. By the church, I'm told. Pretending to be an evacuee.'

'Florrie Wensley? Little Florrie Wensley? I've known her since she was a kid. Family come here every year for their summer holidays. Her husband's in the RAF. She's just had a baby. There's been a mistake . . . I'll ring my superintendent at Bridport!'

'No mistake. She's been sending false telegrams. Creating alarm and despondency. Military censors picked them up. Look!' He waggled a slip of paper.

Millom took one look and turned pale.

LORD GORT MISSING THREE DAYS
STOP PLEASE REPORT ANY SIGHTING
IMMEDIATELY STOP FLORENCE

Hillfield grinned evilly. 'That set the cat among the pigeons in Whitehall, I can tell you. Till they checked Gort was safe. He keeps moving his Army HQ, see? And his communications keep breaking down. The Prime Minister was *frantic*.'

He jerked his thumb towards the church. 'C'mon, Millom, don't stand there all day with soap on your face. There's a war on.'

*

The front lawn of Brereton House was littered with kids' tricycles, balls and tiny red sandals. Through the wide-open windows at least two babies could be heard crying. Florence Wensley answered the door. Sergeant Millom had always thought her very much a lady, but she didn't look a lady this morning. She look a pale, weary wreck; her fair hair was greasy, hanging in strands round her face. She was holding the baby, and the baby had been a bit sick down her jumper. And when she saw Sergeant Millom's uniform she went as white as a sheet.

'Geoff,' she said. 'Something's happened to Geoff.'

Sergeant Millom remembered the husband in the RAF. Flying Blenheims somewhere in France. They said Blenheims were flying death-traps; too slow, not enough guns. They said Jerry was eating them in handfuls for breakfast. They said Geoff Wensley was the last of his old squadron still alive.

And Geoff was lost somewhere in France; like Tom. Millom wanted to say something to comfort her; to say they hadn't come about her husband. But Hillfield took his wrist in a grip like iron, and said coldly, 'Can we go inside, Mrs Wensley?'

The swine didn't care. He was using it to break her up. All he wanted was his spy. A confession.

They went into a front room; pretty once, but faded now, and littered with children's toys worse than the lawn. Florence Wensley sat down in the sagging settee like a falling brick. She was away somewhere inside herself, her eyes blank. The baby, catching her mood, began to cry. Florence's long, pale hands, spotted with drying potato-scrapings, moved automatically to soothe it, like mechanical things.

4

The lines seemed to grow across her face as Sergeant Millom watched. She seemed to wither, turning into an old woman. That's what will happen to me, he thought, when I hear about Tom.

Mrs Wensley made an effort. Her blue-grey eyes came back into focus, like a submarine coming up to the surface, putting up a terrified blue periscope.

'He was only twenty-five,' she said. 'The RAF was his whole life. He was a Regular. He joined up in 1938, straight from university . . .'

Sergeant Millom could bear it no longer. He blurted out, 'It's not about your husband, Mrs Wensley. It's about that telegram you sent.'

She stared at him, turning her head slowly. 'Not dead?' she said. 'What telegram?'

'A telegram about Lord Gort . . .'

She looked bewildered. 'Lord Gort? She's lost.'

Sergeant Millom thought *he* was going mad. '*She's* lost?'

'Lord Gort's a cat . . . Geoff's cat. We got her just when the war broke out. As a kitten. The BEF was going to France, and everyone was talking about Lord Gort. So Geoff called her Lord Gort. We thought she was a tom; but she had kittens. Mummy and I brought her here when we were evacuated from Dover, but she wouldn't settle. She went missing five days ago. We thought she'd go home to Dover. So I telegrammed our old housekeeper to keep an eye open for her . . . has she turned up?'

'Not as far as we know, Mrs Wensley,' said Millom solemnly. He watched life start to drift back into the woman's face; watched her summon up enough courage to ask the vital question.

5

'And Geoff? My husband?'

'We know nothing about your husband at all, Mrs Wensley.'

Her pale smile was the best thing he'd come across in a week. From being ugly, she became pretty. From looking stupid, she became lively. It was like watching Lazarus return from the dead.

'I'm not satisfied,' snarled Hillfield from the corner.

As if in answer, the door opened, and an older woman came in. An older version of Mrs Wensley, but with a nose formed for command and a mouth as impatient as a rat-trap. She was wearing the green uniform and absurd schoolgirl hat of the Women's Voluntary Service. 'God, these evacuee mothers . . .' she said. Then she saw Sergeant Millom's uniform and her face fell apart, too.

'Something's happened to Geoffrey,' she said, flat and dead.

'No, no,' said Sergeant Millom. 'We know nothing about Geoffrey.' He felt as if he were some dreadful plague, haunting the village, tearing people to pieces. 'We've come about Lord Gort.'

The older woman's face resurrected quicker; she was more used to the blows of life. 'Oh, good. Has she been found?'

'No, I'm sorry. She hasn't.'

'Then, why have you come?' Suddenly the older woman became bossy, angry, ready to work off the fright she had had, in rage.

'My colleague will explain all about it,' said Sergeant Millom. 'Goodbye.' He shook hands with both the women, and walked out. Serve the miserable swine right. Let him explain.

After twenty minutes, Hillfield rejoined him, looking furious.

'Thanks for nothing.'

'You're welcome,' said Sergeant Millom.

'I'm not convinced, you know. Calling a she-cat "Lord Gort".'

'I've checked with the neighbours. She's been round the village calling to that cat for five days. Only they thought she was calling "Lord God". They thought she'd gone potty – religious mania – on account of her husband being in France flying those death-trap Blenheims . . .'

'Couldn't care less,' said Hillfield. 'I've wasted a whole day. It's beyond belief, sending telegrams about bloody *cats*. Don't they know there's a war on?'

'Oh, I think they know there's a war on. You haven't got anybody trapped in France, then?'

'What's that got to do with it?' said Hillfield.

Millom just walked away and left him standing there.

Meanwhile, the innocent source of all the panic in Whitehall was moving slowly east, along the high ridges of the downs that overlook the English Channel. A biggish black she-cat with only a few white hairs, invisible beneath her chin. It is impossible to understand exactly what was on her mind. But she was used to having her own way. She did not like noise and upset. She hated the strange house at Beaminster, full of women and children, tears and tantrums. She hated the smells of sour milk and nappies, and the toddlers in every room who would not leave her in peace. She hated the close-packed smells of the Beaminster cats when she went out-doors; cats who attacked her in defence of their own territory wherever she walked.

And she hated the way her own people no longer had any time to stroke and fuss her. She hated the kitchen scraps she was fed, instead of fresh-boiled fish. Above all, she hated the new baby.

She was going back to where she'd been peaceful; where she could spend hours alone, sleeping on the silken coverlet of a sunlit bed in the long afternoons; where she could go to the kitchen and get fresh fish and milk on demand. Somehow, sure as a homing-pigeon, she knew it was ahead.

More dimly – and this was something no homing-pigeon knew – she knew her *real* person was ahead; only further off, *much* further off. She remembered his gentle voice calling her, in the mornings; the tobaccoish smell of his hand stroking her. She remembered riding about on his shoulder, while his gentle hands caressed her. She remembered the game in the garden, when he lay hidden in the long grass, and flicked his white handkerchief while she stalked him. Then she would pounce on him, and they would roll over and over in mock-fury, until the ecstasy of his nearness grew too much for her, and she would scamper off, her back twitching with too much pleasure. To stalk again. And the long evenings by the fire, in his lap, when she would end up lying on her back, paws in the air, and her head hanging abandoned down his long shins.

Somewhere ahead, there was endless happiness again. And she knew how to get there.

Meanwhile, she was not unhappy, merely tense.

She had learnt a few things already. She had learnt to avoid the coastal road, with its endless streams of green army lorries, its vile noise and its vile smell. She preferred soft grass under her feet, and the silence of the Downs, the occasional, widely spaced smells that marked the tracks of other animals, strange cats among them. She paused often, to sniff a sticking-out twig or a tall blade of grass, where another creature had paused to mark its territory. Her ears turned backwards and forwards constantly, assessing every new sound carefully. To her eyes, the world was a fuzzy grey blur, which a human would have thought near-blindness. Only when things moved could she sense them clearly; the flight of the smallest fly caught her eye.

Some sounds and smells would have frightened her if they had not been so far off. She could hear the explosions around Dunkirk far clearer than Sergeant Millom ever would, and not simply because she was nearer to them. She could smell the burning rubber and oil, the smell of the dead, which he would never smell. But far off, so they did not worry her. Nine Hurricanes flew overhead, *en route* for Manston, and then the Battle of France. But she didn't look up; she had long discounted aeroplanes flying overhead. The fat flies buzzing in the hedgerows were more interesting.

She was already in trouble, though she did not know it. Hunger gnawed at her belly. In rejecting the road, she lost the dead rabbits and birds that lay thick on its verges, killed by the passing lorries. She was already hungry enough to dare approach farm-house kitchens; but there were always other cats

9

there, or dogs, or people who threw stones. She had some instinct to hunt, but had never practised it. Instead, she'd chewed a few beetles and spiders. She still weighed seven pounds, but she had been nine when she had left home. Her once-sleek coat was matted with the burrs of goose-grass which her tongue could not cope with.

And her journey was too slow. She did not dare cross an open field; she kept close to the cover of the hedgerows. She wasted too much time assessing every strange sound and smell. She crept along too close to the ground for speed. In five days, she had covered only forty miles. Things would need to change for her, or she would never reach home alive.

She found a dead vole in the next hedgerow; caught and left by a cat from a nearby farm. She mouthed it, then left it. Voles taste vile. A cat will always catch them; but it will have to be *really* desperate before it eats one.

2

In the days following she had no luck with rabbits. She had the instincts to stalk, pounce, bite for the neck, but they were buried too deep in her idle past; they came back too slowly. She hesitated, and was lost. She didn't understand how to use the breeze in her favour; always the rabbits scented her. And she was black, the worst colour for a stealthy approach. She did not keep her rump and waving tail low enough. Always she heard the rabbits' warning thumps, and saw their bobbing white scuts as they went to ground.

Her nearest approach to success turned into the worst. By accident, she approached upwind, so they didn't scent her. By accident, she used the gap in the hedge they had made. She emerged two feet from a baby rabbit, which froze defensively, because it was too close for flight. She gathered herself . . .

Then the rabbits feeding further off sensed her. A crescendo of thumps and the whole group was streaking for safety the only way they knew – back to their burrows through the narrow gap where she stood. She was flattened by an avalanche of brown bodies, some bigger than herself. While she got up, shaking her head to clear it, the paralysed baby rabbit came back to life, and rocketed from under her nose.

As she travelled on, she was limping quite badly

with her right foreleg. By midday she was thirsty and weary. The downland was parched, its streams dried up by the summer heat. But there was a building ahead. The smell of man; a sour, off-putting smell of fear; but also the smell of food.

Stalker rested his big binoculars on the sandbag wall, and rubbed the back of his neck, where the strap cut into it. He was round-shouldered, and getting more so, and the weight of the binoculars didn't help. He hated the long thinness of his body, the bandy legs and sunken chest that were the mark of sub-clinical rickets. The body that had kept him out of the Army: medical grade 3C. The recruiting sergeant had said he was good for nowt, except maybe as a pull-through for cleaning out rifle-barrels. Stalker's face still burnt from the shame of that day, the memory of his own nakedness, the odd pitying looks of the doctors, the guffaws in corners. Civil Defence wouldn't have him either, nor the newly formed Local Defence Volunteers. Too much of a liability . . .

It seemed a miracle when Jones from the Bird-watching Club had rung him up. They needed people for the Observer Corps, to watch for enemy planes from the clifftop observation posts.

Unable to believe in his good luck, he blurted out, 'Do you really want me?'

'Nothing wrong with your eyes, Stalker. Or your binoculars. Can you get to the post above Barton Links?'

He was sure it was his binoculars they really wanted. He hadn't stinted himself with his binocu-lars. Barr & Stroud, the best pair in the district. And

12

he had a car, of course, when some of them hadn't. Barton post was lonely and hard to get to; no close bus service now.

So he'd gone, looking forward to men's company and talk about birds. Lots of the Corps were bird-watchers.

No company. When he'd reached the little sand-bagged hut, it was empty. It had been empty a long time. The notices on the notice-board were bleached into invisibility. The floor was covered with last season's dead leaves. The phone had cobwebs. He was amazed when he picked it up to find that the RAF switchboard still answered.

The reason for its desertion wasn't hard to spot. The post had been built in the wrong place, as so many things would be built in the wrong place in 1940. It covered an area already covered by the advance posts on the Isle of Wight and Portland Bill.

But he came to love the loneliness and the silence, the calling of peewit and curlew, the starlike flowers of the downland grass and the incredible views over the shining sea, from the curving line of Chesil Bank to those mysterious towers at Ventnor in the east. If he met his death, this was where he would choose to meet it; in the quiet of the long summer holiday from school, among the few things he really loved. School had finished early this year; the boarders packed off home when the German breakthrough started in France. Too near the south coast for the Head to take risks. June, July and August stretched barren before him, with Janet tied up in her warm, busy way with WVS and National Savings and evacuees. He had no taste for his beloved garden this year. Too

13

much like hiding away, and hiding away just made you even more frightened.

Frightened of being a Jew.

Not wholly a Jew. Only one-eighth a Jew. His grandparents had solid British names like Jennings and MacDonald, Reeves and Stalker. But he'd had a great-grandmother called Cohen. When the Invasion came, it would come to light. The Nazis took endless trouble weeding out Jews. They would go through the records at Somerset House just as thoroughly as Stalker had, all those years ago, in the search for his family tree. And then would come the concentration camp, the obscene striped pyjamas, the beatings-up and the humiliation of being made to jump through hoops like a circus-animal.

He would kill himself first. He had the little packet of arsenic in his pocket. Not hard to buy, when you were a science teacher. At least it would be quick. Janet would be better off without him. She was all British; he'd checked back eight generations. He hadn't told her any of it. No point in two people worrying . . .

He came out of his recurring death-reverie like a swimmer breaking the surface of a black pool, back into the quiet sunlight. C'mon, Stalker, do your job, your last job. Watch for Nazis.

The circles of his binoculars covered sunlit sky and sea with the absolute concentration he gave everything. Nothing unusual. A small coastal convoy, edging its way past the Needles. You couldn't hear the guns at Dunkirk today. The wind was in the wrong direction. But there was a little dark bird calling, further down the hill. Meadow pipit?

14

A roar of aircraft behind his back. But he knew they were British before he turned. Defiants, with their fat bodies and rounded wingtips. Going to the battle. Heroes. He logged them scrupulously, envy in his heart.

He was sipping tea from his Thermos when he saw the cat limping up the turf towards him. His first thought was that black cats were lucky. But through his binoculars she didn't look very lucky. She looked thin, beaten, furtive, and her fur was staring.

He had no feelings about cats, one way or another. But she was an event in the monotony. Company. When she paused, throwing back her head to sniff, ten yards from the post, he took a pressed-beef sandwich from his packet, and sallied out to meet her. She fled, though he called to her as softly, as gently as he could. He thought bitterly that he couldn't even give a starving cat a beef sandwich properly. He tore up the sandwich and dropped the pieces on the grass and went back inside, watching her through the dark slit that was so much like a bird-watcher's hide. He watched with sad satisfaction as she sniffed and ate the sandwich; then turned his attention back to the sea.

Next thing he knew, she was up on the sandbags beside him, purring wildly, rubbing herself in ecstasy against the hand that held the binoculars. He laughed at his sudden success; his popularity. He gave her another sandwich. That, too, vanished instantly.

He became drunk on doing a fellow-creature good. In all this terrifying world, here was someone to whom he could make a difference. She got the rest of his lunch and tea. He had no appetite; his fear

15

made him feel slightly sick all the time. Janet told him off when he brought back his sandwiches un-eaten. He stroked the cat tentatively, horrified at the way her spine-nobbles stuck out, the sharpness of her pelvic bones.

'Poor old puss. You've had a hard time . . .'

The cat began to purr brokenly, so softly he could hardly hear her. She sat down on the sandbags by his elbow and began to wash herself. Somehow, she made the abandoned post feel fully manned, with a proper garrison. Like home. The afternoon sun seemed warmer. The war in France not quite hope-less. The blood seemed to move in his veins for the first time in a fortnight.

'You stick by me, puss. We'll see you right.'

That evening, when he packed up, he took her home in the car. He'd been scared she might struggle, escape. But she sat on his lap quite naturally, as if she were used to cars, had sat on her late owner's lap in the same way. He thought her late owner must have been a merry, crazy young man, to drive around with a cat on his knee. He felt a bit of a dog himself . . .

Janet gave the cat the rest of the stew they had for supper. Again, the cat ate as if she hadn't eaten for a month. They worked for an hour, getting the burrs out of her coat. It was Janet who made the fuss about the little brass medallion on her collar.

'Lord Gort? D'you think she *belongs* to Lord Gort? There's a Dover phone number. She's a long way from home. You'd better ring them up.'

But the phone just rang and rang, in the empty house on the sea-front at Dover. Stalker was not unhappy to get no answer. He stretched his endless legs across the hearthrug, careful not to disturb the sleeping cat. And listened to the news, read by Bruce Belfrage. The world seemed a little better than it had seemed for many days.

Each day he drove the cat up to the post with him. Janet teased him; but she was glad he seemed happier. The cat threatened to eat them out of house and home, what with the rationing. But she grew sleeker, and ceased to limp. At the post, she would vanish for long periods, practising her hunt for rabbits. She brought her first prey back to him. It was still alive so he drove her off with wild shouts. It died convulsing in his hands, leaving just a smear of bright blood from its neck on one of his fingers. It seemed so new, so perfect, so scarcely begun; the tiny death, linking up with the terror across the Channel, blackened the whole morning for him. He took the rabbit home and buried it sadly underneath the rhododendrons, wrapped in a good handkerchief.

But, by and large, his mood was upwards. He reported more decisively down the telephone, though there was little to report. He chatted up the girl on the switchboard, who had no more to do than he had. He learnt her name was Marge and she had worked in a draper's before the war.

There was, for some absurd reason, a tiny weathered flagpole attached to one corner of the post. He brought the Union Jack from home that they'd bought for the Coronation in 1937. He watched it flutter bravely, and thought sadly of happier times.

In the long sunlit watches, he lettered a red and white signboard to read:

ROYAL OBSERVER CORPS.

With the flag flying, the board up, the Austin Seven parked nearby and the cat washing, the post lost its ghostly look.

And then, on the fourth day, it happened. He'd just been following the progress of another westbound convoy, on an afternoon of exceptional clarity that promised rain, when he raised the glasses and saw tiny dim shapes out over the Channel. He thought at first they were gulls, but their formation was too rigid.

They had drooping gull-wings, though. And only one kind of aircraft had drooping gull-wings. The silhouette leapt into his mind's eye, out of the aircraft-recognition manual that he knew by heart.

Junkers 87s. Stuka dive-bombers that had blasted their black way through the newsreels from Spain to Poland, Holland, Belgium and France. Hitler's terror-bird that turned armies into fleeing rabble. Nothing could stand up to the Stuka. It was always the beginning of the end . . .

I must be dreaming, he thought. Eyes playing tricks. He had lost the faint silhouettes. He refocused desperately and found them again. Watched them grow nearer, paralysed as in a nightmare.

Then he grabbed the phone. Talked of vectors and angels, estimated distance and gave numbers in a calm voice he didn't recognize and which certainly didn't belong to him. To his amazement, Marge took him seriously, though there was a gasp as she absorbed the shock of it. Nothing like this had ever happened to either of them before. He heard his message being taken up by other female voices, as if it were being sucked into some vacuum-cleaner, getting bigger and bigger all the time.

He hung up the phone and raised his glasses again, terrified that the shapes wouldn't still be there; terrified of being in trouble, getting laughed at for giving a false alarm. But the gull-winged shapes were there, larger and clearer now. Turning towards the crawling coastal convoy. From being afraid for himself, he became afraid for the helpless ships.

It was like the time he'd watched a spider trap and eat a bluebottle. The same cold inevitability; the same insect efficiency; the same feeling of helplessness, of being outside, of not understanding. He saw the Nazi squadron-leader waggle his wings, and the first dive-bomber lift a little and then plunge. A bit like a tern diving for fish . . .

Tiny shellbursts in the sky, as the leading ship opened fire. Hopelessly off target. The bomber pulling out in a graceful curve, echoing the curve of the tiny bomb towards the second ship . . . a slowly growing column of white water, as the bomb missed. Then the delayed sound of the bomb bursting, rolling across the quiet sea.

Then the second bomber diving, and the third. They seemed so casual, taking their time. They couldn't go *on* missing . . .

There was a sudden roar over his head, coming so suddenly it made him jump out of his skin. A tight wedge of brown planes shot into view through his observation-slit. Brown, therefore British. Single-engine fighters. Pointed wings, therefore Spitfires . . .

He watched the two groups of planes closing, willing the Germans not to see their danger till it was too late. Hands clenched, sweating, he felt great waves of hate and rage bursting out of him, through his eyes, through the binoculars, as if he had a deathray inside his head.

The two groups of planes met, with a noise like a boy running a stick along metal railings. Then they exploded into a whirling cloud of planes, weaving meaningless patterns, like midges at sunset. Then a long plume of smoke across the sky, like a brush-stroke spreading on wet paper. Not a British plane, oh, God, let it not be a British plane on fire! No. As the plane turned in its death throes, he saw the hated gull-wings.

Another growing brush-stroke, and another. All German, something was fearfully and wonderfully wrong with Hitler's devil-birds. They were dying all over the sky. He heard a voice yelling and screaming and shockingly blaspheming. A mad voice that called for death and blood and burning. He realized with a shock that it was his own. All the fear and hate of weeks streamed out of him.

It was as if he was overheard. A gull-wing was coming straight at him, the noise of its screaming engine growing like a railway train coming through a station. He saw his own death coming. He never saw the British plane behind, until he heard again, louder, the noise like the sound of a boy running a stick across railings, and the sandbags in front of him exploded into his eyes and he was blinded.

*

He kept on hearing the cat mewing querulously, as if she wanted feeding. He pulled out his handkerchief, and tried to get the tears and sand out of his eyes. The hanky smelt of oil from the car.

All was silent. With still-streaming eyes, he went outside. Out to sea, the convoy crawled on, unharmed. There wasn't a plane in sight. Until he looked behind the post.

It lay there, quite close, with its nose dug in the turf. It looked as big as a house, the black crosses shining with varnish on the pale green undersides of the wings. It had dug up the turf like a plough; the exposed chalk was half muddy, half creamy white. One of the plane's wheels had collapsed; it was resting on its big round bomb, still in place.

He didn't know whether to run to it, run away, or phone the switchboard. But something made him walk towards it, though he knew it was a foolish thing to do. He walked up under the towering tail; looked up at where the rear-gunner should be. All he could see was the round holes in the metal; the metal was all buckled and shiny where the bullets had knocked the paint off. The tail looked like a colander, it was so full of holes. And red seeped from the holes. A drop fell on his hand, and he licked it and it tasted of blood, like when you cut your finger.

He went round slowly to the front, dreading what he would see. But the pilot was alive, just sitting there with the cockpit-cover back and his goggles pushed up on his helmet, smiling to himself as if he were relaxing on the beach. There was a frightening smell of petrol. Liquid dripped on to the steaming engine, and evaporated with a hiss. He knew the

21

plane was going to explode at any moment. He knew he should turn and run. And the pilot just sat there, grinning mildly and stupidly, as if he had all the time in the world . . .

'Come on,' Stalker shouted. 'Come *on*!'

The pilot waved a gloved hand at him idly, as if to some casual acquaintance.

Then Stalker went mad. He tried to scramble up the wing, with the metal slithering, scrunching and buckling beneath his feet. He grabbed at the pilot's shoulder, to stop himself falling. There was a harness holding the pilot in. It was supposed to have a release-button somewhere in the middle of it, but he couldn't see it. In his frustration he ripped the pilot's helmet and goggles off, and slapped him on the face.

'Ja, ja!' said the pilot understandingly, as if not offended. Then he seemed to get the idea, and pressed the release button for himself; at last the harness slipped off him. And somehow Stalker hauled him out, and the pair of them did a mad waltz on the crumbling wing and slithered off on to the turf. Stalker grabbed at something painfully hot, and hauled both of them to their feet; he only realized afterwards that his hand was badly blistered. Then they were running and staggering towards the post. Stalker pushed the pilot in, shouting, 'Lie down, lie down!' And grabbed the phone and got the switchboard.

Then the world fell on him.

'Just you lie there for a moment, sir,' said the policeman. 'You've had a nasty shock, the plane blowing up like that.'

22

Stalker stared around wildly from his place on the turf. The post was a tumbled heap of burst sandbags, and where the plane had been was just a vast shallow white crater. But his Austin Seven was still on her wheels. Didn't seem a scratch on her, apart from a crack across the windscreen. They said bomb blast did funny things.

The Nazi pilot was lounging against the Austin's front wing, making it bend. Smoking a cigarette and eyeing a bunch of silly land-girls, who were pointing pitchforks at him vaguely and giggling as if they fancied him. He was the typical Nazi, tall and broad and Nordically fair, even with a cleft in his chin. He looked perfectly at home, taking his pick of the land-girls, with an arrogance that would have made Stalker hate him even if he'd been an Englishman.

Stalker felt deeply ashamed, lying there on the turf, making a fool of himself in front of everybody. Everybody would be laughing at him in a minute, even the Nazi.

But the Nazi came across to him. (The land-girls fluttered nervously.) The Nazi bent over him, took him by the hand, pulled him to his feet, slapped him painfully on the back and hugged him like a bear.

'Mein Freund. Mein Freund.' Stalker never forgot the pressure of the Nazi's hand.

'He seems very attached to you, sir,' said the policeman. 'Saved his life, did you? Get him out of the plane before it blew up?'

'I didn't seem to do anything, really,' said Stalker.

'I reckon you're a bit of a hero, sir,' said the policeman, as flatly as if he'd been charging Stalker with some minor motoring offence. 'Now we'd better get down to the station, sir, if we can use your car. I'll leave my bike here, for the moment. Do you feel up to driving, or shall I?'

Stalker stared round at what had been his post of duty. The Union Jack was in ribbons; the painted board lying on the turf twenty yards away.

'There was a cat . . .' he said fearfully.

'In the car, sir, waiting to go home. Crafty little sod.'

Stalker drove, the cat on his knee. He was very muddled, and occasionally the car swerved a bit. But he didn't feel afraid any more. All the things he had feared – bombs, death and Nazis – had *happened* to him now and he felt deliriously happy.

Janet and the doctor kept him in bed two days, fearing concussion. Word got around, and half the town of Eastleigh seemed to call to see him. His last visitor was a shy young airman in uniform: the sergeant-pilot who had shot down the Stuka. He didn't look half so impressive as the Nazi. Short and a little tubby, with the faint ghost of a moustache, he looked young enough to be a sixth-former. He recognized Stalker instantly as a schoolmaster and it became just like talking to one of the boys at school. The pilot started calling him 'sir'. He told Stalker that the Stuka was his first confirmed kill; it seemed absurd that such a boy should kill anything. They fell to talking about which university the boy was going to after the war . . .

As he rose to go, Stalker said timidly, 'That one you shot down . . . Was it my phone call that alerted you?'

'I don't know, sir . . . We get all our instructions from our controller over the radio.'

The next morning, when Stalker was allowed up, they told him the cat was gone.

3

She came to the hole in the fence above the railway cutting and paused, one foot in the air, sniffing suspiciously at the smell of soot and oil. It reminded her of the roads she hated, of huge things rushing past with a hot wind that knocked her off-balance.

But she smelt water, too; and she was thirsty. She picked her way carefully down through the darkness; sniffed the first metal rail and crossed it to the shallow tank that ran beyond. The water in the tank was oily, unpleasant, but she drank, and sat down and gave a few desultory licks at her fur. She was hungry again, and weak with it. She had still not properly got the trick with rabbits. The only thing she had touched all day was the flattened black corpse of a crow, lying in the dust of a side-road. And that had been mainly feathers that fluttered in the wind, as if wishing to come back to life again.

It was at that point that she smelt the food. It was five yards away, hidden in the long grass of the embankment, but she found it. Half a sandwich, with three bites taken out of it. The white bread and margarine she disliked; but the corned beef was good.

No sooner had she finished it, than she smelt another, further on. And another, and another. She became fussy, pawing apart the bread to reach the meat.

There were other things, as she trotted along: cigarette packets, an empty French brandy bottle, a cap with a regimental badge, a bloody piece of bandage. She sniffed at them without understanding; she sniffed longest at the vile bandage with its whiff of corruption.

She had covered nearly quarter of a mile, sniffing and eating, when the railway lines on each side of her began to vibrate. The sharp gravel beneath her paws began to shake; and then she heard the rumble ahead and saw the pin-points of light like eyes, gleaming in the dark.

She crouched; but as the lighted eyes widened, as the roaring black bulk around them grew, as the rumble turned into a hissing and a roaring, she remembered the crashing Stuka, and fled up the embankment like a black streak.

The train passed; and she returned to the endless trail of food. The train had left behind new smells; blood, sweat, urine and again the disturbing smell of human fear. But the night was still again, and she trotted and ate, ate and trotted.

When the station came, it made her pause. It seemed to be in darkness, but inside there was the sound of women's voices; many women's voices, busy, urgent. And there were dim cracks of light round the blacked-out windows. And the smell of food; lots of meat.

She crept nearer, up on to the sloping end of the platform, towards the door from under which came the smell of food. Then the door opened suddenly, sending a streak of light across the dark, empty

27

platform, revealing a row of milk churns, a wicker basket.

'And another box of marge, George,' said a woman's voice, bossy but weary.

'Right,' said the man standing in the door.

The smell of food was now overpowering. The cat slipped past his legs and in.

Her first impression was of many other legs, women's legs. Stout legs in baggy slacks or lisle stockings and strong sensible country shoes. Legs that shifted constantly to ease themselves, as if the feet hurt. Above, from the tabletop came the sound of bread being sawn into slices, the slither of buttering, the scrawk of tins being opened. And among the legs, from the tabletop, dropped a constant rain of crumbs of bread and meat. The cat slipped silently under the table, and began to lip up the meat with a questing pink tongue.

Above her, the voices went on, unheeding.

'I'll never be able to look a tin of corned beef in the face again.'

'You go home and wash your hands . . . but if you wash them a dozen times, you can't get the smell of marge off them. I can't *stand* the smell of marge.'

'Makes my old man fancy me. He *likes* the smell of marge. Gets all amorous . . .'

'*Amorous?* Fine time for that. Haven't had me corsets off for a week. Just sit in the chair a minute, an' I'm snoring. He's having to see to hisself, this week. A sandwich widower, he calls hisself. Says I'm starting to *look* like a sandwich.'

'Ladies,' said the bossy female voice. 'I thought

you'd like to know we've just made our nine thousandth packet of sandwiches.'

All the women looked at a blackboard at the end of the room. The only woman in the whole room in a hat stood there, a piece of chalk in her hand. She had just added '9000' to a long line of crossed-out figures on a blackboard.

The stout women all put their hands to their aching backs. There was a murmured cheer.

Then the man opened the door again, and said, 'Next train's due in ten minutes. Just gone through Ashford.'

The cat beneath the table felt the atmosphere change. From being cosily weary, the atmosphere grew scared, expectant. The women began taking off their flowered pinafores, and putting on their flowered hats.

'Got to look your best for them!'

'It's the ones who won't stop crying that I can't stand. I mean, they're safe home, now. You'd think they'd cheer up.'

'Shell shock it is . . .'

'I don't reckon half of them will ever fight again.'

'Mrs Barstow,' said the bossy woman, sharply, 'that's *treason*. The Germans are doing well enough without your help. Careless talk costs lives.'

'Old bitch. What does *she* know, up at the Red House? They're only workin' lads. They done their best. It's them stupid generals . . .'

'Them lads is *lions*; lions led by donkeys . . .'

'That will *do*, Mrs Barstow!'

'We got a crate of beer here . . .'

'No alcohol,' said the bossy woman. 'How often

29

have I told you? *No* alcohol. Tea or coffee, sandwiches and cigarettes. But only five cigarettes a man. We've only got two thousand left, till the Service Corps get here in the morning.'

Trolleys were wheeled in and wheeled out again, laden with great steaming urns and mountains of greaseproof packets. The cat followed.

Outside, a pink dawn was breaking; a cold dawn wind blew past the rows of milk churns, making the women's skirts flutter. The train was a plume, then a blob, then it was pulling in. There was nobody looking out of the windows.

A woman pulled a carriage door open, then recoiled at the stench, wrinkling her nose.

Oil. The floor and seats were shiny with it. Great smears and handprints covered the doors and windows. Eight men lay slumped, shiny and black with it, faces and uniforms, so they looked like bronze figures from some bleak and desperate war memorial. Rifles were stacked at their feet, with steel helmets on top.

'Are they *dead*?' asked a woman nervously.

'Just dead tired, love,' said another. 'Wakey, wakey, lads. Char's up. Gotcher mugs?'

The nearest man opened his eyes, and stared blearily. 'Bloody hell – women! And fags. What's this station? The Pearly Gates?'

There was a stir and a fumbling. All sorts of receptacles were held out: mess-tins, china mugs, glasses, all thick with oil. Oily hands reached for the cigarettes, breaking them in their eagerness, mauled the neat packets of sandwiches. Teeth bit in like sharks', startling white in the black faces. Whites of eyes, rolling everywhere, like the eyes of terrified negroes. Then one of them said, 'Christ, look, a bloody black cat. That's the first bit o' luck I've seen since Abbeville . . .'

And suddenly they were reaching out, stepping on to the platform to touch the lucky black cat. She backed away, scared of the oily hands.

Then a voice yelled, nervously, angrily, 'Get back on the train, lads. Everybody back on the train. You know the rules.' It was a huge military policeman, immaculate in red hat and white webbing. There was a pistol in a white holster at his belt; for some reason the flap was unbuttoned. The soldiers got back inside, like scared dogs yelled at by their master.

'Wotcher call the cat, missus?'

'Don't know.'

'He's got a medal on his collar . . .'

The woman picked up the cat timidly and looked at the medallion.

'Lord Gort,' she said.

One man started laughing. Then they were suddenly all laughing. It wasn't ordinary laughter. It wasn't very nice laughter at all.

The guard blew his whistle. The train pulled away slowly, leaving the empty tea-urns, the greaseproof paper blowing along the cold morning platform, the women just standing, as if dazed.

'Come along, ladies. There'll be another train in half an hour!'

'What they *done* to them?' whispered one woman. 'What're they *doing* to them over there in Dunkirk?'

The cat stayed four more days.

The cat met every train.

*

Sergeant Millom turned in through his garden gate.

There was a pair of filthy black boots on the front doorstep. Army boots. He broke into a run, opened his front door, scarcely daring to breathe. There was a new smell in the house. Smoke and oil, as if a paraffin stove had gone wrong.

'Tom?' he cried. 'Tom?'

No answer. He pushed open the living room door. There was a rifle lying in the middle of the hearthrug; a full set of webbing with ammo pouches slung over the back of the chair. A pair of stockinged feet, with enormous holes at toe and heel. The sound of a profound snore.

Sergeant Millom looked at his son's face. He couldn't have washed his hair in a month. Filth was engrained round his eyes. He looked like a dirty twelve-year-old, back from football. His mouth was open. His fingernails, on the arm of the chair, stuck out a quarter of an inch, and were black.

Sergeant Millom just hovered there, thinking what a totally marvellous place the world was. He wanted to do good to everybody for the rest of his life.

Tom opened his eyes and smiled. 'Hello, Dad. There was a black cat on the station. Where we stopped for sandwiches. It was called Lord Gort. I knew I was going to make it home, when I saw the black cat.'

Then the tears began to run down his cheeks. He wasn't crying; the tears simply rolled down his cheeks, as natural as little streams running down a hill. Sergeant Millom grabbed him and hugged him, as he hadn't done since Tom was eight.

Tom had seen the rats, all right. But the black cat

had saved him. When he let Tom go, the lad just fell back in his chair and went fast asleep again.

Sergeant Millom tiptoed around the house, not knowing what to do next, so full of gladness he felt he might be sick.

He'd go down to the butcher's and get a bit of steak for Tom's tea. The butcher wouldn't stint a lad back from Dunkirk . . .

Going to the butcher's on his bike, he saw Mrs Wensley out with the baby in the pram. He pulled up. He saw her face go pale, so he called out, 'Good news, Mrs Wensley!'

Her face lit up. 'Geoffrey?'

Then he felt ashamed; the news about Lord Gort seemed such a poor thing to offer. But she kept a grip on herself and just said: 'Headcorn station? That's on the Dover line. She *is* going home.'

He fled, before the tears came.

After the fourth of June no more trainloads of troops came from Dunkirk. The women packed up their tables and urns, and went back to their husbands. The cat, who had become a legend, became a nuisance instead. Her endless supply of corned beef dried up. She missed the fussing of the women, the admiration of the soldiers. The station-master and the two porters were too busy and too weary to pay any attention to her. She began to go hungry again.

When a train of soldiers pulled up at the down-platform on the tenth of June, it must have seemed to her that her great days had returned. She jumped off the platform and crossed the lines, narrowly missing death under the wheels of an up goods-train.

But the soldiers she found were very different soldiers. Nervous, but not terrified. Clean, with new equipment. Soldiers going back to the front line, which was now Dover. Soldiers with old rifles from the Great War, borrowed back from the Home Guard.

She wandered into a carriage through an open door. Strong warm hands picked her up. 'Who're you, then, pussy-cat?'

He looked at her medal.

'By God, lads. She's called Lord Gort and she's female. That explains a lot . . .'

The soldiers guffawed, a bit too loudly. They were nervous of the Germans; but they were far more nervous of their new Geordie sergeant. He was a tall, thin man, with a big black moustache, and tattooed arms. He'd survived Dunkirk. They thought him slightly mad. He'd taken a Luger pistol off a dead Jerry, and they said he lay in bed and trimmed his toenails by shooting bits off them with it. They said he was bomb-happy, after seven days on the beaches. They said he didn't give two buggers for anybody, British or German.

They'd not seen battle; they were fresh from training in Scotland. He was just what they needed was Sergeant Smith.

The train gave a jolt, as a hint that it was going forward. The cat tried to leap off the sergeant's knee and out of the carriage. But he held her by the scruff with a firm hand, struggle though she might.

'Ye're our luck, pussy-cat, and by God we're going to need it where we're gannin'.' He looked at the other side of her medal. 'Besides, we're going your way – Dover.'

A porter came past, and slammed the carriage door. As the train began to move, the cat relaxed on the sergeant's knee. She had again that dim sense that she was going in the right direction.

She arrived at their billet on the sea-front inside a half-emptied kitbag. There'd been a bad moment when she'd miaowed plaintively while the platoon were being inspected by Major Brimsby. But Sergeant Smith had said quickly, 'That's odd, sir. I could've sworn I heard a cat miaow.' And several soldiers had sniggered, and the Major had moved on quickly, before trouble developed. The troops were pretty touchy, after Dunkirk. Best pretend there was nothing happening . . .

Mrs Smiley, on whom they were billeted, heard the miaow and wasn't so inhibited. She opened the kitbag, lifted the cat out and said, 'Oh, you poor thing!'

'Regimental mascot, ma'am,' said Sergeant Smith, with a very straight face.

She gave him a hard look. She was afraid she was going to have trouble with Sergeant Smith.

Sergeant Smith gave her a bland look back. He had a feeling he wasn't going to have any trouble with Mrs Smiley at all . . .

The cat was left with Mrs Smiley during the day, with strict instructions that she was not to be let out.

'But I thought she was your regimental mascot?'

'We haven't time for her, in this emergency, madam. But we rely on you to keep her safe.'

Mrs Smiley examined the collar, and rang the number on the medallion several times over the next few days; but she never got a reply. She decided to bide her time till she did.

On the fourth day, Lord Gort escaped out of the open bathroom window. She trotted swiftly along the sea-front. She knew she was nearly home.

Here was the beloved gate, the familiar front door. The smell of the housekeeper, quite strong; the smell of her mistress, much fainter; the smell of her master, very faint indeed. But home.

She hung around for a long time, getting hungrier and hungrier. She was not to know the housekeeper only came once a week, now. Worms and beetles from the garden were not very sustaining.

Eventually, she despaired of ever getting in. She made her way down the cliff, through the massed coils of barbed wire, very carefully, and on to the beach that was now a minefield. A cat-loving, steel-helmeted sentry on the clifftop called out a warning, unavailingly. Watched, heart in his mouth, as she stepped over every mine without hurt, and made her way through more coils of barbed wire to the sea.

At the edge of the waves, she stopped, shaking her wet paws. She knew that somewhere ahead was her person, but far, far away. She miaowed plaintively; stood staring at the moving blur of uncrossable sea.

Then she made her way back to Mrs Smiley's house, and a very warm welcome. For the time being, she would be patient.

4

All the soldiers were sitting down to dinner in the kitchen when the cat arrived. She jumped up among the dirty plates, sniffing hopefully here and there, then walked along to the sergeant, who sat at one end. A dozen hands reached out to stroke her, but it was to the sergeant she went.

'You won your bet, Sarge,' called out one young soldier. 'She came back.'

'Course she came back to me. She knows what's bloody good for her.'

Mrs Smiley watched the sergeant's hand stroking the cat. He had big hands, but well shaped, with long, slim, clever fingers that now twisted the cat's ears, now gripped her by the nape of the neck, now dug along her twitching back like a living comb. Mrs Smiley could almost have sworn he was hurting the cat, except the cat was purring loudly and rubbing her cheek against his clever hand in ecstasy. How strange, thought Mrs Smiley, that ecstasy should be so close to agony. A cold draught seemed to come under the kitchen door, and caress the backs of her own legs. She shivered, unaccountably. Silly, it was a warm night really . . .

The sergeant gave the cat a chop-bone off his plate. She ate it on the table, while his hand still caressed her. Mrs Smiley didn't really approve, but it would have been silly and petty to make a fuss. Especially in view of what followed. The sergeant knocked for silence with the end of his unused dessert-fork. 'I want a word with you lads . . . No, don't get up, Mrs Smiley, I want you to hear this, too, so nobody can say they didn't understand . . .' He glared around from under his fine straight black eyebrows.

'I have noticed sand on the stairs. I have noticed beer bottles under beds. I have noticed a fag burn on a dressing-table that wasn't there yesterday . . .'

There was the beginning of a snigger that his glance silenced instantly.

'Now I want to say this. Mrs Smiley is a *lady*. And she didn't ask to have ten ignorant squaddies billeted on her without warning. But she's done her best to make us comfortable, you'll all agree. Now what I'm saying is that she has enough to put up with, what with her husband being in the army in Egypt, and her house on the sea-front about to be blown to buggery by those bastards across the Channel. She doesn't need beer bottles lying about and sand on her stairs and fag burns on her dressing-tables and God help the bastard responsible if I catch him. And you will watch your effing language in front of a lady, and you will address her at all times as "madam". She is an officer's lady, and you will treat her as such. An' if she asks you to wash up, there will be no breakages, or they'll be docked from your effing pay, an' if she asks you to go to the shops or sweep the path, you'll do it pronto, PDQ. Right? Thank you, ma'am. Brody and Corporal Siggis are on washing-up rota this week . . .'

Again, Mrs Smiley shivered. How had the sergeant

found out that Donald was an officer in Egypt? She hadn't told anybody. And he was rough on the cat, but the cat loved it; and he was rough on the soldiers, and the soldiers loved it. He was full of controlled violence; savage-tongued. But he was no fool, by anybody's standards; less of a fool than some of the officers she had met. And his battledress was as thin and well tailored as an officer's; quite unlike the great bulging blanket-like hairiness of the others'.

He sensed her watching him. 'Is there anything I can do for you, ma'am? I don't want you soiling your hands. I'll send one of the platoon along to give you a hand at three o'clock every working day – make a change for them from fillin' sandbags. They'll peel spuds – anything you want. I'm angling to get a lad who was a cook in civvy street, but I think the Officers' Mess has got wind of him.'

He came and stood beside her; too near for her comfort. He was so tall; and always aquiver with tension. And yet he seemed to enjoy everything he did . . .

'You happy in the Army, Sergeant?' It seemed a silly thing to say. Who could be happy these days?

'The Army's my mother and father, ma'am. Three square meals a day, and no need to wonder where you're going to sleep. Plenty o' fresh air. Beats being an unemployed shot-firer, hanging round the colliery gates, hopin' that they'll take you on for three quid a week. This war's the best thing ever happened to me. G'night, ma'am!'

Oddly, he had good teeth when he smiled. Only, the gaps between them were quite marked. She wondered whether being an unemployed shot-firer had made them like that.

'C'mon, puss – up to bed. Keep me back warm . . .' He reached over the table, scavenging scraps for the cat, which he held clinging to his shoulder. He piled the scraps on to one of Mrs Smiley's best rosebud plates. She felt she ought to say something, but again it seemed so petty.

The next Sunday, when Mrs Smiley got back from church, the soldiers had gone to their own church parade. They'd left the kitchen spotless, and all the vegetables done for lunch and floating in bowls of water. The potatoes had been mauled rather savagely; great holes scooped out of them so they looked like Henry Moore sculptures.

She drifted up the sand-free stairs, and into the bedrooms they occupied. Again, spotless, the beds made in a hard, stretched, rigid way that made them look like hospital beds not in use. Up in the attic, where four of them slept on the bare boards, the blankets were piled in perfectly square blocks, with another blanket folded round them, on top of the hard half-mattresses that looked like biscuits and they called 'donkey breakfasts'.

Sergeant Smith had the smallest bedroom for himself; it was just as rigid as the rest. Not a personal belonging in sight. Curious, she opened the wardrobe door, and blushed. The inside of the wardrobe door was plastered with photographs of pale naked women, standing absurdly in rural settings of rocks and ferns. The women looked . . . lost . . . as if they didn't know what to do with their bodies, as if they'd been ordered about, arranged artificially by the man who took the photographs. She supposed they must do it for money. She wanted to turn away, but she kept on staring. Their bodies were slim and beautiful . . .

She'd been as slim as that when she married Donald. But she'd put on weight slowly but steadily, every one of the ten years she'd been married. She still played tennis at the club every summer; but the waistband of her long white skirt had got tighter and tighter. She'd let it out, and needed to let it out again.

She closed the wardrobe door swiftly, and went downstairs to her own room. Stared at herself in her own mirror. Thought: I'm twenty-nine, and I look forty.

She decided to polish the silver on the dining room sideboard. Polishing cheered her up when she felt depressed. She worked on a copy of the *Daily Telegraph*, spread over the dining room table. The dining room, with its silver candelabra, felt icy-cold, even though it was the height of summer. She hadn't used it since Donald went away; the soldiers always ate in the kitchen.

She kept on thinking of the lost naked women, fastened up with their rocks and ferns, inside Sergeant Smith's wardrobe. How could they *bear* to do it, knowing that any man could pay sixpence for one of those magazines?

To banish the thought, she went and got Donald's last letter, three weeks old.

Yesterday, I went to draw the Mosque of Mohammed Ali. Big and nasty – a Victorian

41

attempt to copy Santa Sophia. A little Arab boy hung around me for all of an hour, hoping for baksheesh as usual. I'm afraid he waited in vain! But I enclose a drawing of him. He tried to look so pathetic and hungry in one of the dirty little nightshirts which they all wear out here.

They think at HQ that the Italians might come into the war soon, on the side of Jerry, now Adolf *seems* to be winning. So there might be a bit of trouble with the Eyties on the Libyan frontier around Sollum. I don't think there's much to worry about if they can't show better form than they did against the tribes in Abyssinia, but our regiment –

The rest of the paragraph had been cut away; the jagged edge showed traces of the censor's blue pencil. The regiment must have gone somewhere dangerous . . . She could still not believe that Donald was an officer in charge of four medium tanks. He looked slightly absurd in the tiny photographs he sent, leaning against a tank, deliberately casual, a cigarette in his hand. His knees under the baggy shorts would have gone a painful pink with the sun; his balding head would be peeling amidst its ring of ginger hair. His red face clashed horribly with his ginger hair when the sun caught him. She remembered their last holiday at Torquay . . .

He was the last man to be in a fight; unless it was a fight to save one of his beloved ancient buildings. He should be back home in the office, at his drawing-board, designing semi-detached villas.

With a sigh, her hands returned automatically to

cleaning the silver. Her eyes went past the lace curtains of the dining room to where the milkman was coming down the road with his horse and cart. Donald was not a happy soldier, bravely though he pretended. Not like Sergeant Smith . . .

The dining room door was ajar behind her back; she could feel a tiny warm draught blowing in from the hall. Suddenly the draught got stronger, as if someone had pushed the door open. She whirled. The cat was standing there, staring at her. By this time she disliked the cat strongly. It was Sergeant Smith's cat. It had time only for him; although she had all the bother of getting fish-heads and boiling them up to feed it. She had come to hate the evil burning smell of the boiling fish-pan, the dribbles of white foam that dripped down the side.

The cat miaowed in a dreadful dire sort of way that Mrs Smiley had learnt meant one of only two things: that it was going to be sick, or that it had caught a bird. In either case, mess. Mess on her poor carpets. So when the cat turned and trotted urgently back through the door, she hurried after it.

But the cat stopped at the cellar door, which lay nearby under the staircase in the hall. Pawed at the door urgently. Still frightened it might be sick on the hall carpet, Mrs Smiley opened the door for it. Far better for it to be sick in the cellar. The cat vanished into the dark.

At the same time, Mrs Smiley heard a plane pass very close overhead. A single-engined fighter from the sound of it. *Very* close. Too close for safety. The front door shuddered with the closeness; the brass plaques on the wall made a tinny sound against the oak panelling. The RAF messing about again . . . she wondered if she should write to her MP about it.

She went back into the dining room. There was another loud noise; like somebody hammering nails into a board with a very heavy hammer. What *could* the neighbours be doing? There seemed to be *three* of them hammering now. The hammering had a funny wide echo.

She looked out of the window. The milk-cart was nearly halfway up the road. The milkman came out of a gate and whistled to the horse. The horse began to walk towards him, with a rumble of iron wheels, and a clop, and a tinkle of bottles. The milkman reached into the cart for more bottles . . .

The low-flying plane was coming back . . . even lower this time.

There was a noise like a boy running a stick along a row of metal railings. The milkman looked over his shoulder towards the sound. Then he was running towards her house, mouth open, milk bottles dropping from his arms.

The milk-cart seemed to explode; the milk shot up in a column as high as the top of the new lamppost. The brown horse fell down in the shafts. The milkman fell on his face.

Direly, the cat miaowed again from the cellar door.

Some inner part of herself made Mrs Smiley dive out into the hall and down through the cellar door. She tripped; fell down the last five steps. As she lay, elbows and knees an agony, there was a terrifying crash of glass upstairs. A shower of things fell on her back from the cellar ceiling. Then again the plane passed low over the house, seeming to shake it to its foundations.

And then, as she lay there dazed, she heard the air-raid siren go.

She picked herself up, and stared about her. Some-body had chopped a long hole in the cellar ceiling; ragged ends of lath and plaster hung, lit by light trickling down from the dining room above.

Bemused, she heard the siren sound the long, unbroken note of the all-clear. She wished they would make their minds up. She climbed the stairs feeling very weary; the cat kept on rubbing against her, as if wanting to be petted. It nearly tripped her up; she yelled at it angrily.

She forced back the dining room door, which seemed to have swung to. And stood unable to move.

The windows were gone; the curtains were blowing out through the jagged edges, tangling and tearing themselves. But, more amazingly, the dining room table lay tilted together in two halves; somebody had chopped it in two. All the silver she had been cleaning lay in the valley in the middle, knives and forks like a shoal of shining fish. On top lay a battered chunk of metal, torn into a kind of silver lace. She had to pick it up before she recognized her coffee-pot. She only recognized it by the handle . . . There was a long hole in her carpet, with the darkness showing underneath. The musty smell of the cellar came up to her, with the acrid smell of spilt 'Silvo'. The wall was covered with great pale stars where the plaster had burst out through dangling strips of her best striped Regency wallpaper . . .

What had done it?

Then she realized that whatever had done it had passed straight through the spot where she had been standing cleaning the silver. But for the cat . . .

Where *was* the cat? Was it hurt?

But it came walking sedately out of the hall, sniffed the wreckage carefully, then sat down and began to wash its shoulder.

She remembered the milkman. She ran outside. There was the same long deep kind of hole running across the lawn from a narrow gap in the privet hedge. There were little silver mushrooms scattered all over the lawn. She absently bent and picked one up. It was very heavy for its size. She put it in the pocket of her pinafore. She only realized later that it was a machine-gun bullet, flattened from hitting the brickwork of the bay window.

The milkman was not where he had fallen. He was further up the road, bending over his horse, among a little crowd of people who were gathering. She could see the horse's head and neck, sticking out, through their legs. The head was moving, trying to lift itself . . .

Slowly, she walked up to the little crowd. She was terrified of what she would see, so she kept her head down. The surface of the road was pitted with a long line of little holes that led straight as an arrow to her fence, her garden, her dining room. Dozens of the little silver mushrooms . . .

She reached the back of the crowd; saw their legs. Heard the milkman sobbing, saying things between sobs.

'She's the best horse I ever had. She knew her

own way back to the stable. Oh, God, fetch a vet somebody. I can't bear watching her suffer . . .'

Mrs Smiley just stood, feeling weary beyond belief. Back turned to the crowd and the terrible breathing of the dying horse. Staring at the tea-roses peeping over Mr Marshall's fence, the same as they did every year.

Rough hands grabbed her by the arms.

'Thank Christ you're safe!'

She knew who it was before she looked up. She felt so upset about the milkman and his horse that she nearly fell against him and wept. But one did not cry in the street.

There was the returning roar of low-flying aircraft. Next second, she was lying flat on her back, with him on top of her, arms wrapped tight around her.

She felt surprisingly safe . . .

'Bloody Hurricanes!' spat Sergeant Smith with disgust. 'Bloody RAF. Always too late. Just the same as Dunkirk.' He pulled her to her feet and dusted her off with solicitous hands, as she turned away shyly and watched the three brown planes roar off over the Channel at full boost, superchargers whining.

'Surely the RAF performed wonders over Dunkirk?' she said sharply, cross.

'That what the papers said? Oh, the Brylcreem Boys'd come over and knock down one or two. Then they'd go home to tea with their floosies in the mess, an' leave us for two hours to get bombed.'

She walked by his side back to the house, stiff with indignation. The rest of the soldiers trailed behind at

47

a respectful distance. He saw the damage and whistled. 'Lucky to get out of *that* alive.'

'It was the cat . . .' She told him all about it, though her teeth chattered and she was starting to shake all over.

'That cat's as wise as any Christian . . . they should make her a bloody officer. Corporal Siggis! I want you to take this lady for a walk. Take her for lunch in the best hotel you can find – you can afford it. Don't bring her back till five o'clock.'

Washed and changed, and oddly reluctant to argue, she let herself be taken off by Corporal Siggis. Siggis was the odd one out, a public schoolboy, very tall and handsome, but painfully thin and looking about sixteen.

'I only got my stripe because I applied to be an officer,' he said with engaging honesty, as they sat finishing a rather mediocre lunch. 'The rest take the p— mickey out of me, when the sergeant's not there. But the sergeant says I'll make quite a good officer when I start to shave . . .'

'You seem very attached to the sergeant,' she said, sharply.

'Oh, he's the greatest. Up in Scotland, our lorry went into a ditch. The platoon-commander hadn't a clue what to do. Just stood there looking at it, and nibbling the end of his stick. He's a bit of a twit . . . ex-bank clerk. Then Sergeant Smith said, "Shall I carry on, sir, while you go and phone H Q?" And we had that lorry back on the road before the platoon-commander had walked a mile. I hope when I get my pip I'll have a sergeant like him. They carry the whole army, the sergeants.'

'How very fortunate for you,' said Mrs Smiley with even greater sharpness. She was wondering if Donald had a sergeant carrying *him*. She was also having strange and unwelcome memories of the sergeant's body enclosing her.

It did not help when Dolly Linden came drifting across the restaurant and said, 'Hello. Who's your little *friend*?'

'My nephew, actually,' said Mrs Smiley icily. 'On leave. From *Dunkirk*.'

'I say, you don't care much for *her*, do you?' said Corporal Siggis, admiringly, staring at Dolly's departing back.

'She's normally a good friend of mine,' said Mrs Smiley, furious at the mess the imperious Sergeant Smith had landed her in. 'Do you normally take ladies out to lunch at your own expense, when Sergeant Smith orders you to?'

'Oh, *anything*. He's the tops. Stood on the parapet at Dunkirk for four days, taking pot-shots at Jerry bombers; with only a rifle. They say he ought to get a medal, but he won't because officers don't like him.'

'I wonder why?' said Mrs Smiley, in a voice calculated to form ice on the half-full water-jug. 'And just what is he getting up to in my house, I wonder?'

They arrived back at precisely 1700 hours, as Corporal Siggis quaintly put it. He kept her hovering at the end of her own street for the last ten minutes, under the censorious eyes of passers-by, who thought

49

that mature wives should not be seen out with soldiers young enough to be their sons . . .

Not only was the glass of the dining room window replaced, but it was sandbagged to a height of six feet. Empty sandbags lay about, and the flower-beds had sunk about a foot, to the great peril of her roses. The hole in the lawn had been turfed over, and the hole in the hedge trimmed to look artistic.

Inside, the dining room floor had been repaired with a new plank, and an old rug brought out of storage in the attic to cover the newness. The tall sideboard had been pulled round to cover the bullet scars on the wall. The shattered table had gone, replaced by an old pine kitchen job that had appeared out of nowhere and was stamped 'WD'.

But the biggest change was in the cellar. It had been reinforced with criss-crossed heavy beams overhead, held up by a network of steel posts.

'Stand anything now but a direct hit,' said Sergeant Smith. 'You'll be as snug as a bug in a rug.'

'And who is going to pay for it all?' asked Mrs Smiley.

Sergeant Smith squeezed her arm, conspiratorially. 'Your good friend and mine, King George the Sixth. You look after him; he looks after you.'

The cat leapt on his shoulder, and began to lick the inside of its foreleg.

King George continued to be a good provider as summer passed. It was not the bags of potatoes that worried Mrs Smiley, nor the loaves of bread. It was the seven-pound tins of butter; the endless cigarettes that were thrust at her.

But she began to take the cigarettes, though she had never smoked before. The Channel opposite Dover became known at Hellfire Corner. Attacks on passing convoys and on the town became commonplace. They said the Germans were building giant guns on the Pas de Calais that would be able to *shell* the town.

But every evening those who were not on sentry duty gathered for dinner in her kitchen. Mrs Smiley at one end of the table and Sergeant Smith at the other, with the cat on his lap eternally reaching up a black paw for titbits that were never refused. Like Mum and Dad and one big happy family. The light was on in the kitchen all the time now because the kitchen window had been sandbagged by Sergeant Smith as well. There were said to be steel plates covering the joists of the loft, to protect the house against shrapnel from the ack-ack guns. There were red buckets of sand lined up along the hall. Mrs Smiley had long since ceased to think of it as *her* house.

She was too busy, anyway. The vicar had asked her to run a canteen in the church hall. Because he had heard that she was good with young soldiers. The first night, as she locked it up to come home, she was surprised to be met by Siggis and Hall, who fell in one on each side of her.

'What's this? Prisoner's escort?' she asked, mildly alarmed.

'Sergeant's orders,' said Siggis, rather embarrassed. 'He says where there's soldiers, there's *women*. He doesn't want you to be mistaken for one of them.'

'That's very kind of the sergeant, I'm sure,' said

Mrs Smiley. She had given up being icy. It just didn't seem to work in wartime . . .

But when they passed a guard-tent pitched on the cliffs, they saw a couple of girls hanging round it, chatting up the soldiers inside and giggling. Mrs Smiley knew them, from church. They couldn't have been more than fifteen. She spoke to them sharply and told them to go home. She would speak to their mothers tomorrow. They seemed to obey.

But when she turned to look back, at the end of the sea-front, they were back in the same position in the dusk.

'It's the war, ma'am,' said Siggis apologetically.

Hall started a snigger, but stifled it hurriedly.

Mrs Smiley herself had lost half a stone in weight. She was sharper, tenser, made sarcastic cynical jokes. She had given up having permanent waves; she was letting her hair grow into the new pageboy style; she was not above admitting she was 'browned off' occasionally.

She got whistled at in the street by soldiers. She never acknowledged the whistles, but they helped carry her through the day.

5

The cat clawed at the blackout curtain over the door, and they let her out. She paused on the doorstep, to accustom her eyes, her ears, her nose, to the sights, sounds and smells of the night. Then she leapt the garden wall, and set off round her circular walk. It was the same walk every night. It never varied, except perhaps for a diversion of ten yards to anything new or interesting.

The Army would have said she passed through three zones.

The first was the zone of love. The zone on the inland side of the defences. Here, on a fine warm night (or even on a stormy one), the courting couples lay thickly clustered; in locked-up parks, on miniature golf courses; under the cover of bandstands and seaside shelters, in air-raid shelters and even in the overgrown gardens of the larger houses. In some places they were no more than two yards apart, yet each couple worked hard to preserve the illusion of being alone together in an empty universe, huddled on groundsheets, under army blankets and army greatcoats.

The cat made its way softly through the giggling, writhing, heaving bundles, listening here, sniffing there.

Where there were giggles, there was a chance of

food, a welcome into a shared world of transitory warmth. These were happy couples, well established couples, old friends who would share a sandwich or a biscuit with her, who might even have brought a titbit especially. Little brief families who thought the cat was a heavenly blessing on them, a bringer of luck from the gods of war, an assurance that they would continue, that death would not come yet, to one or the other.

Where there were great heavings, gasps of passion, the cat might wait patiently for them to stop, with a little curiosity shown in the sniffing of her nose, and an ancient timeless stillness that seemed to have known and seen all. She had learnt that passion can be followed by great kindness.

Only at heaped bundles from which came muffled but sharp voices did she not linger.

'Jack, will you swear on the Bible you're not married?'

'I told you. I live with me mum!'

'Then why can't I write to you, when you go on leave?'

'Me mum's old-fashioned. She doesn't like me going wi' girls.'

'But you're *thirty-six*!'

The cat passed on, understanding nothing, yet understanding that there would be neither food nor welcome there.

She passed on to the edge of the zone of danger, marked by the massed coils of barbed wire, the sand-bagged sentry-boxes, the tall, skyward-pointing fingers of the sea-front Bofors guns. Here, again, she

54

used her nose, smelling out those who were kind, who gave her a welcome; and those who were cruel.

She made a habit of accosting the nervous sentries before she began to go through the wire; there were tin cans tied to the wire in some places that tinkled at the least disturbance of the wire. And sentries, made nervous by the great weight of German darkness out to sea, by the unseen shadow of Cap Gris Nez only nineteen miles away, would sometimes blaze away at the slightest noise. There were also sentries who would shoot at stalking cats for the sheer hell of it; but she knew their smell also.

Out into the zone of danger; the minefields. There was food here, too, that rustled stealthily in the dark. Where men no longer dared to walk, wildlife was creeping in; raising second litters of the summer in the peace of the landmines. The mines were no danger to her. It needed a certain weight to set them off, a weight far heavier than the foot of a stalking cat; though foolish leaping dogs had ventured there in daylight, after an ill-thrown ball, to be blown to smithereens.

She came upon the scent of mice, rats, rabbits, weasels, perhaps a fox. Even the foxes didn't worry her. She was fit now, big and heavy. A fox might try an attack, but a sharp claw to his nose would send him yelping. The foxes had learnt; they always backed off first now, even when there was food to be disputed over.

And there was the scent of other patrolling cats. She walked circumspectly there, avoiding quarrels. There was enough prey for all.

And so down through the second belt of wire,

often lapped by the incoming waves, to the zone of death. There could be food here, too, washing limp, dead and relaxed in the foam and weed of the tide-line. Fish, killed yet unmarked by exploding bombs and shells and sea-mines, floating belly-up. Gulls, shot down in bloody ruin by the lines of Oerlikon shells from the convoys that missed a bigger flying prey. Sometimes all fresh and good and bloody; sometimes inedible in a vile-smelling soup of oil from the sinking ships, or fuel seeping from crashed planes lying on the sea-bed half a mile offshore.

Tonight, it was bad; the smell of oil came to her nostrils while she was still inside the second wire. But she went to look, just the same, careful to keep the sucking oil-slicked foam of the waves from her paws. She went to look out of pure curiosity.

At a bigger bobbing shape than usual, floating within its escort of dead fish. The flier had had time to take his helmet and goggles off before he died in the water; time to get rid of his chute. Beyond the vast hump of his inflated life jacket, his long hair floated and swirled in the oily water. His eyes still seemed to glint, as he shook his head sadly with every incoming wave. The cat did not wonder if he was British or German; she was neutral in such matters.

Far inland, beyond the huddling houses, the siren sounded the alert. The cat took no notice. Alerts did not necessarily mean anything unpleasant.

But far off, still over France, she could hear aircraft engines approaching, whose broken, unsynchronised note did mean trouble. She moved back up the beach swiftly, running low to the sand with her tail down.

Long before the first guns sounded, she was back in Mrs Smiley's kitchen, scrabbling at the door that led to the hall and the cellar.

'Trouble, lads,' said Sergeant Smith. 'Time to get below. She knows, you know!'

Down in the cellar Mrs Smiley watched the cat, crouched in Sergeant Smith's lap, twitch in her shut-eyed brooding as the first bombs fell. Sergeant Smith led his troops into the first chorus of a vile song he had filched from the blue-jobs, the RAF.

> Cats on the rooftops, cats on the tiles,
> Cats with syphilis and cats with piles . . .

Mrs Smiley did not join in, as he had known she would not. Sometimes he could be so *sweet*, and other times so *provoking*. But at least the singing kept out the sound of the bombing.

Only one disturbance broke the cat's steady routine. Towards the end of June, she became dimly aware that her master was no longer to the east, across the scary, exciting, blurred, moving mass that was the uncrossable sea. Instead, he was behind her now, to the west. But as far off as ever, faint, dim. She was reluctant, slow to respond. She had a new home, a new master. But on the second day she did set out back to Dorset. Only to become bafflingly aware that his presence was moving rapidly north. And then, within the same day, he vanished out of her ken altogether.

She turned, and walked the six miles back to the billet.

They had become worried, and were very relieved to see her.

Mrs Wensley was out shopping with the baby when she saw the RAF officer. He came limping towards her down the street, and she thought at first it might be Geoffrey.

Then she told herself not to be silly. It was not just that he had one arm in a sling. He was far older than Geoffrey; middle-aged. There was grey in his hair, under his forage-cap. Lines on his face. Far too thin for Geoffrey. And he seemed to hug the wall, keeping his eyes down, not looking at people, as if he were ashamed. He had none of Geoffrey's *bounce*.

Yet he *was* like Geoffrey. Well, more like Geoffrey's father, really. Like Geoffrey's father's younger brother, perhaps . . .

But what had happened to the poor man? He had that bereaved look that men got when they lost their wives. His skin was nearly transparent, and wrinkled too easily, shockingly easily, when he stepped aside to let someone pass, and winced with pain. What a strange young-old man!

'Hello, love!' said the strange young-old man, and tried to smile at her. But the smile broke up halfway.

It was Geoffrey's voice. It was Geoffrey's way of saying 'Hello, love!'

They were Geoffrey's eyes, searching into her own, the way they had always done. The same mole on his cheek.

He held out his good arm.

She flung herself into it with desperation; it was like flinging yourself into the arm of a strange monster, a living corpse masquerading as your husband.

He felt the reluctance in her body; dropped his arm quickly from round her, as if he'd almost been expecting the rejection. Bent quickly over to tickle the baby whom he'd never seen.

'So this is the little shaver . . .' The finger he poked at the baby trembled uncontrollably, like a very old man's, a very old man with that disease . . . Parkinson's.

She said, 'Oh, Geoff, what have they done to you?'

He looked up with a skull-like grin, an attempt at brightness. 'I got wounded. They shipped me out on the last ship that got out of France before they surrendered. Brest. The Jerries had the town surrounded; they fired on us from the clifftop. Bloody narrow scrape. But you know me, darling – lucky.'

'How's your crew?' She somehow knew she shouldn't ask. But she'd always asked about the health of his aircrew before, and she couldn't think of anything else to say.

'Simpson bought it over Abbeville, on the last show. Bowen's in hospital – lost his leg. They had to leave him behind somewhere in France. At the end, you only got away if you could walk. How's your mother?'

They walked home side by side, silent as strangers. She said, 'How long have you got? When are you going back?'

'I've only got a thirty-six-hour pass. Then Northern Ireland, then to Canada via Iceland. I'm going on the Empire Air Training Scheme. They wanted someone who'd flown in battle to lecture on

59

combat tactics. There's not a lot of tactics to flying Blenheims. You fly high, they shoot you up; you fly low, the buggers still shoot you up. I hope they don't give the new kids Blenheims. I hope there aren't any Blenheims left.'

She couldn't think of anything to say. They went upstairs to find her mother.

The next twenty-four hours were the longest in her life. He couldn't sit still for five minutes. He kept on looking at his watch. Kept asking what time the pub opened. She had to tell him six times.

The baby crying got on his nerves; the noise of the other kids in the house got on his nerves. They left the baby with her mother, and went for a long, aimless walk.

Once, he said suddenly, 'They're putting me up for a gong.'

She didn't know what a gong was, and he yelled at her for being stupid, when she asked.

Another time he asked, 'Where's Lord Gort?'

She was very ashamed to tell him Lord Gort was lost. But he laughed when she told him about Head-corn station and Lord Gort heading back for Dover. 'Black cats are lucky. She'll need all her nine lives in Dover.' It wasn't a nice laugh. When they got home again he spent a long time trying to get through on the phone to Headcorn station, and then had a violent row with the station-master. He spent a long time ringing the Dover house, but couldn't get a reply. He talked about getting out their car and driving over to Dover to look for her. Then lost his temper again when she explained about petrol rationing.

Only in the pub on Saturday evening did he regain

some of his old gaiety. For half an hour, she relaxed and was happy. Then he began to get pretty drunk, because everybody wanted to buy drinks for the hero. She got him away before he attacked the government for building rubbish planes a second time.

He refused to go to church on Sunday morning; the first time he'd refused since they'd been married. He had a row with her mother about it that shook the whole house. In the end nobody went to church. Sunday lunch was a meal of black brooding silence. And then he was gone.

She was glad he was gone. She was glad that he'd be safe from the fighting in Canada. They had plenty of food in Canada; plenty of peace. Maybe they'd make him well again.

Meanwhile, she was just glad he was still alive, and glad he was gone.

6

One Saturday afternoon, the siren went about half-past four, but Mrs Smiley kept the canteen open. All the windows were sandbagged now, thanks to Sergeant Smith, who seemed to have an inexhaustible supply of them. Whenever anything bad happened, he seemed to relieve his feelings by sandbagging another building.

The women put on their steel helmets, also supplied by Sergeant Smith; with their flowered pinafores, it gave them a raffish look. They enjoyed them as they might enjoy a new spring hat. The tin hats gave rise to a lot of jokes; they broke the ice with the soldiers. A bit later, Sergeant Smith came in and said the Jerry bombers were passing each side of Dover, keeping well away from the ack-ack guns. Jerry wasn't interested in Dover this evening; he hadn't been interested for a bit. It had been the airfields that had been taking the hammering. But Sergeant Smith told her on the quiet that there were a hell of a lot of Jerries, and he thought they were heading for London. And, as usual, there wasn't a bloody RAF fighter in sight.

The women took off their helmets; they were too big and terribly heavy, and they fell off every time you looked down to pour a cup of tea, or cut a sandwich. They'd broken quite a lot of teacups that way.

Around six, the all-clear went. They all breathed a sigh of relief, and the rate of laughing and chatter went up in the canteen, like it always did when the all-clear sounded. The afternoon helpers went home; and the evening shift came on. One woman said her husband had just come back from seeing his mother in Gillingham. Jerry had gone for London all right. They'd set the docks alight from end to end, and the smoke blowing across the river was so thick and high it had blotted out the sun.

The siren went again at half-past seven. A sort of silence fell, with only the rattle of the urns; and the women buttered sandwiches furiously. They didn't seem frightened, but a lot of them knew somebody who lived in London. Sergeant Smith said the new Jerries were mainly passing south of Dover; there were more of them than ever, and again there was no sign of the RAF.

Dusk fell. Soldiers coming in from duty said the sky to the west was pink.

London was burning.

Mrs Smiley almost wished they were being bombed in Dover instead. It gave her a queer feeling, knowing London was copping it. She kept on thinking about the Houses of Parliament, and the King and Mr Churchill. Suppose they killed Mr Churchill? It would be the end.

Then Sergeant Smith came in, unusually grave, and took her to one side. 'You won't see me for a bit. They've sent "Cromwell".'

She gaped at him. 'Sent Cromwell where?' She

had an absurd picture of Roundhead troopers on horseback cantering through the streets of Dover.

'Cromwell's the code-word,' he said. 'Invasion imminent and probable within the next twelve hours.'

'*Who's* sent it?' she said crossly, because her stomach suddenly sank like lead.

'Top brass. They think Jerry's coming. What you want to do? Go home? Pack up?'

She thought about the cellar at home, silent, the lads gone, only her and the cat. Not knowing what was happening. Sitting in the dark with the light of only a candle. 'I'd rather stay here. I'd rather be in company.'

'Good lass. Ye're probably as safe here as anywhere. I'll try and get word to you, what's happening. I'll send Siggis.' Then he was gone, a new spring and briskness to his step which she envied him.

Then the rumours started. Someone had heard church bells ringing to the west. A despatch-rider had met a landgirl on a big black horse, galloping around the North Downs, looking for parachutists. She had twopence in her pocket, provided by the government, so she could gallop to the nearest phone box and telephone the local Home Guard.

At five past ten, bugles sounded all over the Dover Cliffs. But Siggis came tearing in and said it was a false alarm. On a calm moonlit night there was nothing in sight out to sea, except one of our own convoys slipping past. Then somebody else came in, saying the Jerries had landed at Lydd. Mrs Smiley thanked God Lydd was thirty miles away. Siggis came in and said there were plenty of good British troops at Lydd. They'd set the whole beach on fire with flaming petrol as the Jerries came ashore; the sea was black with German dead.

As if to confirm this, the all-clear sounded. Mrs Smiley kept herself sane by being busy.

In the middle of it all sat the despatch-rider who had met the girl on the horse. He sat in his great motorcyclist's boots, his steel crash-helmet on the table beside him, and a crumpled writing-pad and very crumpled addressed envelope. He kept on licking the end of his indelible pencil; his tongue, stuck out with concentration, was covered with little purple blotches. But it seemed that inspiration would not come . . .

'Trying to write to me girlfriend, ma'am. In case I buy it. But I can't think what to say. She gets nervous easily. I've always tried to write her cheerful letters . . .'

She sat down at the table opposite to him, and smiled. He had a snub nose and a lot of Brylcreemed hair, flattened into an odd shape by the weight of his helmet. He looked about sixteen, like Corporal Siggis. It was easy to smile at him, even when she felt like screaming her head off. She kept wanting to suggest something for him to write, catching in her head at heroic phrases from literature. Sidney Carton in *A Tale of Two Cities*. 'It is a far far better thing that I do now than I have ever done.' Rupert Brooke. The Agincourt speech about St Crispin's Day, from Shakespeare's *Henry V*. 'Some corner of a foreign field that is forever England . . .' None of which the boy would understand. She wondered what *she* would write to Donald, snug and safe in Egypt . . .

'Just tell her how much you love her. She'll like that. Leave the letter with me. I'll see it gets posted . . .'

'Thanks, miss.' The boy grinned at her, a real grin, and settled down to write. She felt better for having solved a small problem, and went and cut sandwiches with renewed gusto.

The cat returned early from her rounds. Her search for food had been useless. Too many people around tonight; little groups that prowled restlessly with shaded torches and much shouting. They had driven the wildlife to earth. Three times she'd been shot at; she disliked the explosions, which were painful to her ears; and the blue balloons of incandescent gas that licked out ten yards from the muzzles of the rifles; the whizz of the bullet and the acrid smell of cordite.

There were no couples spread around the grass; and the sea smelt thick with oil before she reached it. She gave it up as a bad job, and strolled into the house through the back door, which the soldiers had left blowing in the wind. Once in the house, she was in luck. Half a tin of bully-beef left sitting on the table; a half-tin of condensed milk, an open tin of butter. She glutted herself, and went upstairs through another carelessly open door to Mrs Smiley's bedroom, where the bed had a silk coverlet. With feet oily from the beach, she pounded a comfortable hollow in it, and fell fast asleep.

Mrs Smiley was slumped over a canteen table when

Sergeant Smith shook her awake. He smiled, a little regretfully, in the dawn light.

'Bugger all,' he said. 'I've been as far as Eastbourne, and there's bugger all but rumours. Did you know that the Germans have drilled a tunnel under the Channel and have used it to fire torpedoes at Dover? Did you know that Jerry has captured Hawkinge airfield, and are flying bombers off it already? If they have, the RAF blokes at Hawkinge don't know about it, either. Christ, there's little groups of Home Guard all over the coast road. Some of them have assegais from a play that flopped at Drury Lane. Some have got boarding-pikes from HMS *Victory*. Another lot have got one .22 rifle among twenty of them. It's a bloody good job Jerry *didn't* come. It's a lovely clear morning, and the coast is clear as far as the Isle of Wight. Every bugger says the invasion's a bit further west. Maybe Jerry's managed Land's End, but that won't do him much good. I'll drive you home. You going to church this morning?'

She felt an infinite weariness; but an even greater thankfulness.

'Yes,' she said, 'I'm going to church.'

'Think I'll come with you. There won't be any church parade this morning.'

7

'Ye could do wi' a day off,' said Sergeant Smith the next Saturday night.

'How can I take a day off? The canteen . . .'

'I've arranged with Marge and Jean to run the canteen tomorrow. An' Siggis can run things here. And I've arranged transport. There's somewhere I want to show you.'

She sighed and looked at him. She was too weary to struggle. Didn't he ever get tired?

'I'm still going to church,' she said, defensively.

'The best, hinny. Canterbury cathedral. Be ready at 0830 hours.'

She gave in. He couldn't get up to much in a cathedral.

The transport turned out to be a thirty hundred-weight army truck with a canvas roof. The cat hopped cheerfully on to some sacks in the back. Sergeant Smith gave Mrs Smiley an ATS battledress blouse and cap 'to make things look official'. She didn't dare ask where he'd got them, but it was typical of him that they fitted her. She had to admit he had turned himself out beautifully. His boots shone like patent leather, and his brass badge and belt-buckle as if they were silver.

The service did her good; the cathedral was packed with women wearing last year's summer hats and dresses. Most of the men were in uniform. The choir sang so beautifully that she wept a little, dabbing at her eyes surreptitiously while pretending to blow her nose. She told herself it was just tiredness really. She did not care much for the patriotic sermon, which seemed to assume Germany would be destroyed by fire and brimstone like Sodom and Gomorrah. Her eyes roamed around the massive pillars and soaring roof; the ragged dirty tatters of the old battle-standards. How many wars and battles had come and gone while there was endless quiet in this cathedral? That was the *real* sermon; peace everlasting. She must come here more often.

Sergeant Smith sang the hymns he knew in a surprisingly loud and fine baritone voice, which made those women near them in the pews turn round in half-offence. Sergeant Smith gave them his dark sharky smile; it ruffled quite a few. The hymns he did not know left him silent and frowning, as if they were some offence under the Army Act.

They came out into the sunshine to the sound of an organ voluntary by Bach. She was just telling herself how much she missed Bach when she looked at the sky beyond the west towers of the cathedral. A thin layer of cirrus cloud had crept across the blue since they had gone inside, leaving the sun a little weak. But it was not that she was looking at.

As far as the horizon, the sky was covered in a network of black planes. They covered the sky like some precise geometric grid; not one was out of place. It was the precision that was more frightening than the numbers; it cancelled out the English sky, it cancelled out hope itself, like a postmark across a postage stamp. Two cancellations, one on top of the other. Below, the twin-engined bombers; above, the smaller cross-shapes of the fighters.

It was so terrible, seeing them so close to the golden stone towers of the cathedral; they blotted out all the peace and surety she had felt inside. She grabbed for the nearest thing; it happened to be Sergeant Smith's large, warm arm.

'It's all right, hinny,' he said. 'They're not coming here; they're headin' for London.'

As if *that* made any difference; she felt they were heading for her own frail beating heart. Oh, stop them! Can't anybody stop them? She felt that God himself was being mocked.

'If the RAF come,' said Sergeant Smith, 'they'll come out of the sun.'

She stared at the white pale disc of the sun, too veiled to do more than make her eyes water. Or was she weeping? She couldn't see . . .

'Well *done*, lads,' said Sergeant Smith. 'Here they *come*.'

She could still see nothing. But there came that sound of a boy running his stick along iron railings; too far away to frighten her. And then the sky above the bombers was full of the aimless midge-swarming of a dogfight.

'That takes care of the Me 109s,' said Sergeant Smith with deep satisfaction. 'Now, if they hit the bombers . . .'

Behind their backs came a crescendo of aircraft engines. By their steady note they were British.

One German bomber went into a nose-dive. It was

coming down vertically towards the far outskirts of the town.

'Dive-bomber,' she breathed to herself. But the bomber never pulled out. It vanished behind the roof-tops and a great cloud of smoke ascended, followed by a dull crump that set the pigeons wheeling from the cathedral towers.

'Lost his nerve,' said Sergeant Smith savagely. 'That's one way o' committing suicide.'

The screaming sound behind their backs increased. A hundred boys running sticks along iron railings. The straight patterns of the black bombers wavered and broke. Some of them began to climb; some to dive. Then the fat-bodied blue-bellied Hurricanes were among them. It was like watching a hundred road accidents starting to happen at once. There was a brilliant blinding flash as two bombers collided. Then the sky seemed full of sagging burning rags of planes.

'The RAF's learnt a bit since Dunkirk,' said Sergeant Smith, grudgingly. 'They've got the buggers on the run.'

Some of the German formations were still keeping on, heading for London. But many were turning back, weaving desperate arcs to avoid each other. They saw two more planes collide, and fall entangled, like mating flies. Streams of bombs fell from others, on to the countryside beyond the town.

'It's as if they were shitting themselves,' said Sergeant Smith with great satisfaction.

As the last sounds of aircraft engines faded he said, 'Well, I doubt they'll be back today. Let's make the most of it.'

71

When they reached the lorry, Lord Gort peered out from under the engine, warily. 'Trust her to find the safest place,' said the sergeant. 'Look at that engine oil all over her tail. I'll have to give her a bath tonight.'

They drove west, quite a long time. Mrs Smiley was content to flop and watch the white weather-boarded villages flow by. She couldn't stop thinking about the German pilot who had crashed his plane into the ground in terror, before a shot was fired at him; and wondering whether he'd had a wife. The war was a black tunnel, in which they were all together, British and German. In which there was no way out but dying . . . .

Finally, Sergeant Smith stopped and pulled on the handbrake. 'Here we are then. Soledon Hill.'

She sat and let the quiet flow into her; and the cool breeze flow round her face. All she was aware of at first was silence and blueness and distance. They seemed to be on top of the world; lesser hills lay around them, with the sea's horizon showing through the gaps between. The silence and height and blue-ness seemed to feed her, like the first fresh-brewed cup of tea after a night's bombing. Then she became aware of lesser things: the lonely cry of a peewit; three sheep cropping grass noisily, and a five-foot obelisk of concrete sticking up out of the turf.

'Ordnance Survey,' said Sergeant Smith. 'What they call a trigonometrical point. And there's the Home Guard, keeping the world safe for democracy.'

Three figures in khaki overalls were slumped against the wall of a small distant concrete pillbox, eating sandwiches, their helmets on the grass beside them. They waved; and Sergeant Smith waved back graciously.

'C'mon,' he said. 'Let's get away from the war. I reckon they can handle it today.' The cat ran boldly off, sniffing randomly at tall dry tufts of thistle and ignoring others that looked equally interesting.

'She's a country cat, that. Knaas her way aboot.'

Mrs Smiley took her picnic basket from the back of the lorry. Sergeant Smith took his gas mask case, and they followed the cat.

They crossed a stile, Mrs Smiley refusing the sergeant's gallant offer to lift her down. Went along a narrow, green road, lined with deep bracken, and over another stile. Mrs Smiley began to realize there was more to Soledon Hill than met the eye. It was ringed by a ditch; by two ditches twenty feet deep, one inside the other. The curves of the ditches were silky; they had been made a long, long time ago, but they were the work of man.

'Ancient Britons,' said Sergeant Smith. 'Fortified camp. This is the approach-ramp and that's the gate. They knew what they were doin'. Anybody chargin' the gate could be shot at from the right. And they had to carry their shields in their *left* hands. Cunning, that. They even gave the Romans a lot of bother. Though the Romans got in, in the end. Slaughtered everybody, just to teach them not to do it again . . . Nobody's used it since then.'

'Can't you talk about anything but war?' Suddenly, she was blindingly angry with him. But he didn't reply, just strolled by her side whistling under his breath, and watching the explorations of the cat.

At last they lay down on the outer side of the

73

upper ditch, with just their heads sticking above the skyline. The sun was warm on the backs of her legs, but her face and hair were fresh and in the wind. There was a tiny miniature farm below, with a toy farmer herding toy sheep. She reached under the red checkered cloth of her basket, and dug out a Thermos and a rather miserable-looking packet of corned-beef sandwiches.

'Here,' said Sergeant Smith, a little smugly. He was holding out to her a plump roast chicken leg, produced from his gas-mask case.

'How . . .?'

'That lad I told you about . . . him that was a cook before the war . . . he works in the Officers' Mess now . . . He's a good mate o' mine.'

'I sometimes wonder whose side you're on . . .'

'Mine.' He ate his own chicken leg, whistling a hymn he'd sung in the cathedral that morning.

'His chariots of wrath the deep thunderclouds form, and dark is his path on the wings of the storm.'

She ate the chicken leg, feeling only slightly sorry for the officers. He fell silent, and she couldn't think of anything to say. Her body pressed against the dry warmth of the hill; she felt all that ancient mass beneath her; all those enduring years. William the Conqueror must have passed; Napoleon across the Channel. People must have been terrified then; but up here, only the wind, and the grazing of the sheep, and the peewits calling. And as she was aware of the hill, of the soft sound of the wind sighing through the widely spaced clumps of thistle, and making the corn in the fields below blow with waves like the waves of the sea, she became aware of Sergeant

Smith's living body next to her. The thud of his toecaps on the turf, as he changed position; his breathing.

Five black rooks flapped slowly out of a little wood below, and settled in the cornfield, And then, within two minutes, they all flew back into the wood again. Why should they do that? Nature was so mysterious; things happened, and you couldn't understand them; but that didn't stop them happening. Any more than she could stop what was happening to her body now.

'Musta been lively up here in the old days,' mused Sergeant Smith, almost to himself. 'I like to sit up here and think about it. Wasn't like it is now – only a few sheep. There'd be ten-foot palisades then, whole walls of tree trunks. And pretty ripe inside the walls wi' woodsmoke and bones chucked down everywhere, and dogs ... and blokes quarrelling an' getting the old knives out.'

The feelings in her body departed abruptly. She turned to snap at him again, but saw that he'd turned his back and was talking to the cat, which was trying to claw the chicken bone out of his hand.

'Greedy sod. Why don't you go and catch your own? Oh, *tek* it! He threw it at the cat in disgust. The cat crouched over it, growling softly, her eyes never leaving his. How well they understood each other, she thought. How alike they were. Polite while it suited them; but savages underneath. Well, they could *have* each other ...

And then, far off and faint on the wind, from somewhere on the coast, the air-raid warning went. The cat vanished over the crest of the ditch, still carrying her bone.

75

'Want to go?' asked the sergeant. She looked round; it was so peaceful here; so far from the war.

'Nooo . . . ooh. I'm too cosy.' She stretched and relaxed again. And then saw the black dots that could only be planes, coming across the sea.

It was too late to run. The truck and the Home Guard pillbox must be half a mile away. The farm must be even further, and down a breakneck slope, over a small river, through the tangled wood. They could only lie on the open hillside and watch, as the mass of planes grew nearer, larger.

'They're flying a bit more ragged than they were this morning,' said the sergeant.

But he was only trying to cheer her up.

There were a lot more of them, too. As inevitably, as undisturbed as a train or a bus approaching a stop to pick up passengers, they arrived and passed overhead. Because of the height of Soledon Hill, they seemed lower than usual. It was quite easy to see the crosses on the pale green undersides of the wings, the swastika on the tails, the tiny dots of the pilots' heads, the numbers and letters on the sides, the rampant insignia of scarlet dragons and black lightning flashes. Faces looked down on them, pale tiny blobs from gun positions. Guns swung, but not a shot was fired. They looked happy, as if joy-riding. The last passed, heading for London; the sound of their engines faded and died.

Peace returned, the soughing of the wind; but it was a bitter mockery. Sergeant Smith tugged miserably at the tiny blue flowers in the turf.

'I'll take a few o' them wi' me, when I go,' he said.

She had no doubt he would; but it wouldn't do any good. Nothing would do any good.

Already the air above them was German; it was as if the exhaust gases of the bombers' engines had remained to take the heat out of the sun. Soon all this land would be German, too, the sheep below slaughtered for soldiers' feasting. She would have Nazi soldiers billeted on her instead of her boys. A traitorous thought wondered whether she could make friends with them; they too were some mothers' homesick sons. There might even be a Sergeant Schmidt who might look after her when it came to rations . . . If she did nothing wrong, there was no reason . . . the Gestapo might leave her alone . . .

They just sat, unspeaking. The sandwiches she'd brought lay scattered meaninglessly. Wasps came to investigate her two precious small home-made jam tarts, carefully saved for over a week.

The war was lost; there was nothing left to do but run and hide. And she couldn't even summon up the energy for that. Instead, she kept her eyes down and dwelt in the safety of the blue flowers, which did not care if this land was British or German.

And then there was the sound of a plane returning. A plane howling in pain. The sound filled the quiet valley below. And there it was, flying low, one wing down, and a long, thin trail of white smoke from one engine, flowing back along its long, thin body.

'Dornier Flying Pencil,' said the sergeant. 'He's not going to make it.'

The plane passed, almost close enough to throw a stone at, and vanished from sight, around the flank of the hill.

77

Then three bombers, fat Heinkels, with a fat Hurricane lying just behind the tail of the rearmost one, so close Mrs Smiley was frightened they would touch. The Hurricane fired its guns; bits fell off the Heinkel. Wearily, black smoke billowing behind suddenly, it began to twist and fall into the valley beyond the hill. The Hurricane moved up casually to the next Heinkel in line, as they passed out of sight.

Now the sky was full of the sound of returning aircraft. They no longer flew in any kind of formation; the faster overtook the slower in their rush for the coast. There were propellers spinning, slowly in the slipstream. One Heinkel seemed to have no nose left; another lacked a wingtip.

'They've had a rare bashin',' said Sergeant Smith. 'And they never made London – never had the time. And they won't come back in a hurry.'

'You keep on saying they won't come back,' said Mrs Smiley, waspishly.

'The RAF means business, now.'

The next thing they saw seemed to prove his words, in a way that was beyond belief. Two Dorniers, flying higher than the rest, huddled close together, as if for mutual protection. And a Hurricane after them, a burning Hurricane, trailing oily smoke. The Hurricane slowly overtook them, but it didn't fire its guns. It simply gained, till it sat directly above them. Then it sat down on them, hitting them with blows of its wings, like a hen settling on eggs.

The three planes fell apart in ruin, tumbling over and over down the sky, like shot grouse. Just one parachute opened, as the wreckage fell burning behind the next hill.

'That was the Hurricane pilot,' said Sergeant Smith. 'He was ready to bail out; he had his cockpit-canopy open.'

'Shall we go and see . . . if he's all right?'

'We'd never find him – he's miles away by this time. Plenty of locals to see to him.'

'I hope so.' She felt he was very hard-hearted.

No more planes came. There was a sort of aching weariness in the air over the hill.

'Hey, look at that!'

Beneath them, unnoticed before, sat a rabbit. Up on its hind legs, ears upright, eyes staring. They watched for a long time; it did not move.

'Paralysed wi' fear,' said Sergeant Smith. 'Fancy rabbit pie for supper?' He got up, and moved towards it stealthily. Even when he got within a yard of it, it still didn't move.

'No!' shouted Mrs Smiley. Normally, a rabbit would be more than welcome. But she had seen too many deaths this afternoon.

As Sergeant Smith turned back obediently, the rabbit returned to life and bolted.

She smiled at him; pleased to have saved one small life amidst all this death.

She never worked out what happened next. Whether it was the death of the planes, or the life of the rabbit. Or the fact that the shadow of the German planes was gone, and the English air was suddenly as wild as wine. But her body just seemed to take over, with a life of its own. While her mind was a whirling chaos in which Sergeant Smith's body, and the falling planes, and that hymn about the chariots of wrath churned over and over.

She was often to wonder just what had got into her, in the years that followed. But she never regretted it.

When it was all over, the cat came and fussed all over them, purring loudly, as if very pleased with them. Finally, she settled on Mrs Smiley's hip, like the queen of the castle.

Ten days later, she got a letter from Donald. The Eyties had finally attacked Egypt, but been stopped at a dump called Sidi Barrani. Donald had lost two of his tanks and part of his left foot, while trying to rescue one of his chaps from a tank that was brewing up. He was being invalided home. His CO was recommending him an MC, though he'd done damn all to deserve it . . .

Sergeant Smith came to say goodbye long before Donald reached home, with a kitbag on one shoulder and the cat on the other. He had, he said, been posted north to a new unit being trained for special operations, whatever special operations were. From the slightly wild glint in his eye, they promised to be rather deadly. He had never mentioned what had happened on Soledon Hill; never even hinted at it by as much as the flicker of an eyebrow.

She would have liked to put her arms around him, but what with the cat and the kitbag, that would have been very difficult. Besides, Corporal Siggis was with him.

The daylight raids had stopped by then. Although she didn't know it, the most dangerous part of her life was over. She was to miss it, badly.

8

It was a pity Sergeant Smith's train did not go straight through to Scotland. It was a pity he had to change at Crewe. It was an even greater pity that, wartime trains being what they were, he was still slumped in the blacked-out station buffet at half-past ten that night.

He'd been waiting five hours, and Sergeant Smith was not good at waiting; it was the thing he was worst at. If he could *do* something, wangle something, he always felt better. There was nothing to do here except leave the foul tea half-drunk in the cup, roll the bread of the stale sandwiches into balls, and cross his legs one way and then the other.

He had been across the road to the Crewe Arms several times for a drink. But he was not drunk; it might have been better if he had been. Then he might simply have become a bruised but innocent victim. As it was, the drink he had had just got him to the dangerous stage. The landlord of the Crewe Arms, infinitely wise in the ways of drinkers, served him rapidly and with the greatest courtesy. The violence he sensed inside Sergeant Smith worried him a great deal, and he was glad when he could throw the towel over his beer-pumps and call time without having had his public bar wrecked.

The cat, too, sensed the violence in her master. She

lay against his neck, and felt the large fingers grinding
into her fur without cease, and bore the mild pain
and irritation, and kept her patience. All the travel-
ling and noise of the railway had kept her constantly
tense, and she was very tired and just wanted to
sleep. She did not like the noises of the station; the
noisy trains rushing past outside, or the noisy men
within. Her safe place had grown very small. All
she knew in this strange world was Sergeant Smith's
greatcoat, and Sergeant Smith's grinding fingers in
her fur.

Sergeant Smith's mind was in a turmoil. He hated
being between regiments. His regiment was his only
home. He had left all his friends, all his power, all
his snug little schemes behind; he would have the
weary job of making new ones at the far end.

But his thoughts about Mrs Smiley were far more
painful. In his simple mind, there were ladies, and
there were women.

Women did it with you; ladies didn't. He'd had his
share of women; a necessary evil occasionally, when
you got so tense you could burst; when you got so
tense you could've hit the CO in the middle of First
Works Parade, just to have something happen. Then
you applied for a weekend pass and drew out your
accumulated pay and went to London on the razzle.
And if you ended up in a drunken fight, the Military
Police would always dump you back at base, and
you'd lose a stripe for a couple of months, then they
gave it back to you because they knew you were a
natural sergeant. Then it was fine, till the next time
you got tense : . . .

But Mrs Smiley had been a lady. An officer's lady.

And she'd broken all the rules by doing it with him on Soledon Hill. It had turned his whole world upside down. He had thought he would despise her afterwards. But he didn't. He couldn't take his eyes off her smooth hair, her sunburnt arms. He wanted to do it again, and from the shy looks she gave him, he knew she wanted to as well. And he'd become afraid for her, in the bombing, like he'd never been afraid for anybody in his life. He could hardly keep his mind on his duty for worrying about her. It made him a bad soldier. It also made him begin to wish that Captain Smiley would buy it, out there in Egypt, so that after a decent length of time he could marry the widow. He had wished the death of some poor sod who was only doing his duty cooped up inside a dark smelly tank in 108 degrees in the shade. Sergeant Smith disgusted himself.

So it was only a just punishment when Mrs Smiley suddenly announced that Captain Smiley was coming home a hero, minus a foot but plus a well earned MC.

He couldn't stay after that, of course. He couldn't bear to stay and watch her with him. So he'd applied for this special operations lark. It sounded pretty dangerous. But by that time he was so blackly miserable that the prospect of being killed with honour seemed the only solution.

But he missed her horribly. And who would keep her safe in the bombing now? Aah, the whole world was a pointless shit-heap.

It was at that point that six blue-clad members of the RAF Regiment came in. A nasty lot; so nasty that their CO had at last got them posted to another airfield. The sort that any wise CO tried to get posted the moment he clapped eyes on them. Barrack-room tormentors; extorters of pay from homesick raw recruits. Sellers of RAF stores to the Black Market, though it could never be proved. They too were tired and angry at being posted away from a cushy billet and their fiddles.

They had their own brand of low cunning, but they were not sensitive to the inward thoughts of men. They only saw the sergeant's shining brass and boots, and despised him for them. Because his legs were inordinately long, he looked rather small sitting there. They thought he looked lost and woebegone. Above all, they had the RAF's contempt for a 'brown job'.

And of course they saw the cat on his shoulder. Animals were good to torment; anything unusual was prey to them.

Two of them drifted across to him; the rest sat watching keenly. Suddenly the day did not seem quite so bad . . . a bit of fun before their train to Blackpool . . .

One of them said, 'I like your cat, Bill!' He bent forward to stroke the cat, who flinched away. He deliberately let the mug in his hand slop tea on to Sergeant Smith's neatly pressed trousers.

It was to Sergeant Smith's credit that he said once, quietly, 'Go *away*!'

'Sorry, mate, did I splash your trousers?' The RAF man, sniggering, bent down as if to brush it off, and spilt some more scalding tea right into Sergeant Smith's crotch.

Sergeant Smith threw him through the frosted-glass

window of the buffet. It had been a rather fine window, dating from Victorian times. The flying body took the blackout curtains with it. The other RAF man was so surprised he just stood there gaping. Sergeant Smith punched him in the stomach, and then, as he doubled up, in the face. He staggered right across the floor back to his mates, landing on his back on the table they were sitting at, sending boiling tea in all directions.

Then all five waded into Sergeant Smith, two picking up bottles as they came. A fierce joy seized Sergeant Smith. From being unbearably complicated his life became beautifully *simple*.

He had three on the floor before the MPs from the station control-point swarmed in. He was using his fists beautifully, and his highly polished boots even better. The trouble was, he could no longer distinguish friend from foe. Everyone who got in his way was an enemy . . .

The Provost Marshal, strictly a realist, finally stopped him by drawing his revolver and pistol-whipping him from behind. It still took three blows to finish him off. They dragged him off to their control-point, and the Provost Marshal fished the movement order out of Sergeant Smith's battledress pocket, and rang the phone number on it. Funny sort of outfit. What the hell were special operations?

He got the CO at the far end. A colonel, though he sounded much too young to be a colonel. The Provost Marshal explained the situation; that Sergeant Smith would be rather late arriving, after a district court martial and several months in the glasshouse . . . The other end exploded.

'Good God, Captain, I *need* that man. We're prac-tising blowing things up, and the man's an explosives expert. I need him *now*, not in three months' time. There's a bloody war on. And if he's got the wit to lay out four RAF idiots and two MPs single-handed, then I need him so much the more. Now, you will get him on the Glasgow train without fail tonight. PDQ. With or without MP escort – I don't give two buggers. You need an authority? Will Lord Lovatt do?'

The Provost Marshal hung up, and wondered at length and with curiously intricate blasphemy what the Army was coming to. Then the Glasgow train came in, and the MPs slung Sergeant Smith aboard, still unconscious.

He came to, north of Carlisle, on the floor of the guard's van. A sympathetic guard, who had suffered from MPs in the Great War, gave him a seat by the stove, and a brew thick with sugar and condensed milk.

'My kit? The cat?' mumbled Sergeant Smith.

'Your kit's here, mate,' said the guard, shoving it forward with his foot. 'Didn't see no cat. It's a joke, is it? Kitty-cat, like?'

Sergeant Smith gave him a look that froze his bones to the marrow.

The cat crept out of the wrecked buffet as they were trying to sweep it clear of glass, out on to the cold, wet platform. The rain was coming down in rods, and blowing in gusts under the canopy, making the whole platform a wet mirror. But she could still smell which way they had taken her master. She followed, but reluctantly, feeling the gusts of rain on the tips of her fur as small twitches in her skin. She *hated* getting wet; she had been wet too often, these last months. She shook each paw in turn, indignantly.

A train rushed past, scaring her into a corner. On the wooden stairs leading up to the footbridge, she was shooed by another group of half-drunk soldiers . . .

She got there in the end, just as they were loading him aboard the train. She started forward, with a silent miaow.

The door slammed on him; the guard's whistle blew. The engine ejected long clouds of steam across the platform with a terrifying hiss.

Before she could move again, the rumbling bulk of the dark train was moving. She watched it dwindle into the night. Another gust of rain sprayed onto her from the canopy overhead.

Wretched, she found shelter for the night under a porter's trolley, piled with crates.

By morning, Sergeant Smith was so far away north, she had not the heart to follow. She sat wondering what to do. And as she sat, a violent storm of tiny movement broke out inside her body, making her bend her ears back, and stare at her belly wildly. She had quite forgotten that encounter with a black tom, on the mined beach at Dover . . .

She set off back towards Dover, so far away, through the rainswept autumn streets of Crewe.

9

Old Ollie had the cart loaded with trusses of straw when the cat came walking boldly across the farm-yard towards him. Bold? Or was she desperate? She had a bulging belly, but the rest of her was as thin as a stick. There were streaks of mud on her black sides.

'Going to have a load of kittens soon,' he said to the farmer.

'I'll drown the bastards. An' her, too, if I can catch her. There's a bloody plague o' cats. Coming out of Birmingham to get away from the bombing. I've shot ten this year, but you can't get the ammunition. It's all going to the bloody Home Guard. I don't know how they think farmers can manage . . .'

'Yeah. My old cat went missing after the last raid, even though it was nowt much. Mind you, she was fifteen; she might have died o' fright. She's a sad miss; she was a right good ratter. This one any good?'

'How the hell would I know?'

The cat gave the farmer a wary glance. Then she gave Ollie a long, profound one. Then she walked round the horse, to the side away from the farmer, and jumped up on the wooden seat of the cart, next to Ollie, and gave him a deep, confiding look.

Once a stray cat looked at Ollie that way, he was

lost. Been that way all his life. Cats were like people to him.

'I'll take her. Any cat's better than none. The rats we got . . .'

'Prefer terriers meself. That's four pound for the hay.'

Ollie clopped off home in the dusk. It still felt odd, pushing a horse and cart through all the rush-hour flow of lorries and buses flooding out of the new industrial estates. He hated the long sheds where they made cars and refrigerators and electric fires. They covered the fields where corn had once grown, with their huge, cocky, garish names. The Daimler works in Sandy Lane, Vickers-Armstrong, Hawker-Siddeley, Rolls-Royce aero-engines, Courtauld's parachutes, Morris motor-engines. The workers seemed to have money to burn from all the overtime. He wondered if they were happy in their neat little semi-detached houses with their labour-saving kitchens and big posh radio sets.

He kept on heading for the old part of town he'd always known: the spire of the cathedral, the narrow-packed wooden houses and cobbled streets, the livery stable he owned, like his dad and grandad before him. Pity he had no son to leave it to . . .

But probably if he had had a son, he'd have been taken up with these new-fashioned things. They said horses were finished; that soon the world would be full of tractors and lorries. But since the war started business had been all right. Petrol was short, but hay wasn't. The horse was coming back into its own. Every time he was called out to pull in a car or lorry that had broken down, he was a pound the richer.

Horses didn't break down, if you fed them right. And you could sell all the manure to the new allotment-owners. And all the kids wanting hay and corn for their rabbit clubs. He was getting quite a little nest-egg laid by, for when he finally retired. Not that he felt like retiring a bit. He might be sixty-seven, but he felt *fit*. And Stevo who helped him was only a young lad of sixty-three. He must look after Stevo. The stables were Stevo's whole life since his missus died. He cooked a treat, did Stevo. Had had to learn when his missus was ill so long . . . And look at old Sampson there, clopping along steady. Didn't give a damn for cars and lorries, old Sampson, though some of the other horses got nervous.

The cat sat beside him, tense, quivering. She hadn't bargained for this, the noise of the traffic, the close tight walls of the houses. She disliked towns and cities. But the man was friendly, and the kicking in her belly made her desperate for food and warmth and dark.

They swung in through the deep arch of the livery stable. The noise and petrol fumes fell back; it smelt like the country. She felt happier.

Stevo was peeling potatoes when Ollie walked into the kitchen. He had a burning fag balanced on the edge of the sink, but it was sodden with being picked up and put down, and it wouldn't burn much longer.

'They're all back and seen to,' said Stevo. 'Trojan dropped a shoe. I'll take him round to the blacksmith in the morning.'

'That's the third shoe this week . . .'

'It's the war . . .'

'Anything on the news?'

'Them Greeks is still chasing them Italians.'

'Italians is rubbish. They wouldn't fight in the last lot, at Caporetto. Just want to go home to mama and the bambinos.'

Ollie had had to clear up after the Italians at Caporetto. It gave him an authority talking about the war. Stevo had been with the army in France, but he'd just been a hoss-handler with the Service Corps at Boulogne.

'What's for supper?'

'Irish stew.'

Ollie grimaced. It always seemed to be Irish stew these days. Stevo had a great cast-iron stewpot that was never empty; he just threw fresh meat and potatoes on top of what was left from yesterday. Said it was called 'pot of fur', and all the Froggy women had done it when he was in France. Ollie suspected that some of the fur was really mould . . .

'Gotta cat.'

'Looks more like you got six cats there. Couldn't you do better'n that?'

'Grimston was going to drown her.'

'Ye're soft, that's your trouble.'

The cat, trembling, tense, nosed round the dark little kitchen. The cupboards whose doors would no longer shut, they were so full of stuff. The long table, piled at one end with towering mountains of newspapers that were supposed to come in handy one day but never did. The shelves lined with dusty bottles that held medicines for men and horses. The mantelpiece over the never extinguished fire where Stevo did all of his cooking, summer and winter. There was an Ansonia wooden clock on the mantelpiece that ticked and chimed and never told the right time, but was good company. And a tin tea-caddy that frequently fell off the shelf because there were so many letters stuffed behind it. Two wooden rocking-chairs, one each side of the fire, each with a large red and purple knitted blanket in it that did duty as a cushion, rug or shawl, depending on the coldness of the weather. The old men often told each other they were as snug as a bug in a rug.

The cat, having nosed into every corner, sat on the grey, ash-laden rag rug that had been Ollie's mother's, stared at the pot of fur, and mewed hopefully.

'Give her what's left,' said Ollie, with malicious satisfaction.

'A hungry cat makes the best ratter . . .'

'Only thing she'll catch, the state she's in, is pneumonia and die.'

'What'll we have to eat, then?'

Ollie reached into his pocket and produced a ten-shilling note with a flourish. He felt rich; he'd beaten Grimston down from four pounds ten to four pounds for the hay. 'Go and get fish an' chips. We'll eat 'em out of the paper an' save washing-up. I'll go and see to Sampson.'

The cat finished all the pot of fur, then followed Ollie back into the yard. It was cobbled, with buildings on all four sides. At night, with the gate shut, as good as a fortress. Along two sides, cart-sheds and the stables, each with a half-door and a massive head looking out. Above, a row of round holes; the lofts where hay was stored. On the third side, the entrance tunnel and the house. On the fourth, the huge barn, empty these days, apart from the great wooden boxes where the grain was stored.

The ARP wardens borrowed it for their barn-dances. Ollie liked to go and watch. The band varied from week to week, depending which local musicians were on leave. The only steady member was Maisie Sutton, the band-leader who could thump the old piano so loud that once they'd never heard the siren nor the bombs dropping. Ollie liked to see the young girls in their pretty frocks sitting on the grain bins sipping American ice cream soda straight from the bottle and swinging their legs. There were still decorations up from last Christmas, mingling oddly with the old harness hanging on the walls.

The cat walked past where Sampson was being seen to. Sampson raised a hoof and clashed it down on the cobbles, sending out a shower of tiny blue sparks.

A warning. There would be no friendship there.

She passed, and stared up at the massive head protruding from the half-door three boxes on. The gentle head of Trojan. Trojan was *too* gentle a beast. Whereas Sampson stamped on the rats that invaded his stall, killing many and trampling them into a bloody pulp, Trojan stood quiet while the rats nibbled at his very hooves.

Trojan and Lord Gort stared at each other a long while, the horse turning his head to one side for a better view out of his large, dark, gentle eye. He batted his ears, in a pattern even the most experienced horseman could not have quite understood. The cat moved her ears forward and up, and gave the softest of mews. Then she gathered herself and leapt on top of the half-door, balanced precariously for a second, and leapt down inside. Then up into the hay of the scarcely used manger. She settled comfortably, her eyes closed.

A lasting friendship was forged. Feeling safe for the first time since Crewe Station, Lord Gort slept.

A rustle in the straw awakened her. It was still night, and the top of the stable door was closed against the cold. A human eye could have seen nothing. But Lord Gort's eyes, dilated as wide and black as a camera lens, picked up movement below.

A brown rat came in through a hole in the door, searching for dropped grain from Trojan's nosebag. It stood on its hindquarters, sniffing the strange smell beyond the smell of horse-droppings, beyond the smell of leather, straw, hay, iron rust and man. The smell of cat. But it was a young rat, grown up since the old cat had gone missing. It discounted the smell, dropped back to all four feet and foraged on through the straw.

Trojan shifted uneasily as the rat crossed his rear hoof. But he did not wake from his standing sleep.

The cat felt . . . threat. As she had never felt threat from the mice, voles or rabbits she had killed. This thing was invading *her* space. Her safe space, which she had needed so badly since the kicking in her stomach began. She got up and stepped with all four feet on to the rim of the manger, balancing delicately.

The young rat raised itself on its hind legs again, alert. But it still did not understand the menace in the smell of cat. And the stables were full of rustles in hay and straw . . . It went on beneath the manger.

Like a black thunderbolt, the cat dropped, biting for the neck. Missed. The rat scrambled for the safety of a corner, where its back would be covered. It was not afraid of the new black beast. It half-raised itself, yellow jaws bared, capable of a very nasty poisoned bite. A bite that would turn septic . . .

The cat did not risk jaw against jaw. She raised her left paw and struck the rat's head between the ears, over and over like a boxer, as fast as lightning. The rat, confused and dazed, ran for the safety of another corner. Again the cat leapt for the neck and missed. Again, the rat reared up, threateningly, jaws open. Again, the flurry of blows from the black paw. Now the rat was so dazed and confused, it ran hither and thither through the straw.

The end came.

The great hooves of Trojan moved uneasily, as the horse smelt blood.

In the morning, Stevo, yawning, opened the house door and trod on something soft. He peered down, blearily. He'd been to the pub after supper, drinking to what the Greeks were doing to the Italians. Though, as the beer flowed, the things that the Greeks would be doing to the Italians had got more and more fantastic, and more and more indecent, until the landlady had threatened to throw Stevo and his cronies out. Then that song;

> Hitler has only got one ball,
> Musso, he has none at all . . .

Stevo, smiling reminiscently, peered down and saw a row of five rats stretched out neatly on the dirty doorstep.

He called upstairs, 'Shuy's keeled. Shuy'll do. Shuy's a ratter.'

Ollie, coming downstairs with his braces still dangling in loops round his trousers, smiled complacently.

'Told you. There's no ratter like a pregnant queen. Vicious, they are. Frightened for their kittens, see. Rats'll take kittens from the nest.'

That autumn was a hard time for rats and Italians. Swordfish torpedo-bombers crippled half the Italian fleet off Taranto. Ollie and Stevo went to the pub and celebrated so well they had to be helped home by a respectful young policeman, who kept rabbits, and knew where to come for his hay and corn.

'My ambition, Constable,' confided Ollie, 'is to live longer than Hitler. And Mussolini. I'm sixty-seven, but I feel I've got more future than them buggers. We're saving up, Stevo and I. After the war, we're going on our foreign travels. And do you know where we're going? We're going to Germany, to Berchtesgaden, and we're going to dance on Hitler's grave. All day an' all night. Then we're going to Italy, to dance on Musso's.'

'Not sure I won't join you, sir,' said the constable with feeling. He peered down at their doorstep. 'What's them? Rats?'

'Nine,' said Ollie. 'That's the best she's scored yet. Tell you what, Constable. I've got the best bloody ratter in the whole of Coventry.'

And, indeed, Lord Gort's performance was

prodigious. There should not have been a rat left in the stables. But the town centre of Coventry was very old. Tall, half-timbered houses clustered close, leaning together over narrow cobbled streets. It was rather like London had been, just before the Great Fire. A rat's paradise. And so, drawn by the spilt grain from the horses, the rats kept coming.

Lord Gort had her kittens in Trojan's disused manger; in the far corner where the hay was musty and not fit to eat. Otherwise, Trojan's great square yellow teeth might have slaughtered them unawares. And, oddly enough, Lord Gort had reinforcements for the birth. That last day she turned up in the yard with another cat, an old black-and-white female whom Ollie immediately called Skinny.

'Do we need two cats?' asked Stevo lugubriously. The Greeks hadn't been doing so well, the last few days.

'The rats we got, we could do wi' ten,' said Ollie. 'Besides, she's the midwife.'

'The *what*?'

'Didn't you know that mother cats had midwives? Old females, who sit wi' them, and help wi' the kittens? Cos they come so fast, the mother cat can't get them free of their sacks fast enough. You mark my words. You watch. She'll go in that manger, and she'll sit wi' her, till her time comes.'

'Ye're pulling me leg . . .'

'Like to bet ten bob on it?'

'Done! You lying old . . .'

After tea, they went out to the stables to look. Lord Gort was lying on her side, in a collapsed sort of way, belly as huge as a mountain. And the other cat sat with her, washing Lord Gort's ears thoroughly. As they watched, Lord Gort began to pant, and they could actually see humps moving, disturbing the fur on her monstrous belly.

'We've just about got time to have supper,' said Ollie, jovially.

They had just got back in the stable, leaving the washing-up, when the first kitten came. The panting Lord Gort gave a heave, and a twitch of her back legs, and something lay on the straw: a coiled-up shape with closed eyes and flattened ears, inside an oval shape of what looked like thick cellophane. On the end of a string. The whole thing not much bigger than a well-grown mouse . . .

Lord Gort peered towards her own rear end. But Skinny was quicker. She pounced and tore at the tiny object with her teeth . . .

'She's *slaughtering* it,' squealed Stevo.

But suddenly the transparent envelope was empty. The tiny creature was pawing at the hay, weakly. Skinny pounced on the pink string and chewed through it awkwardly with the side of her teeth. Then she was licking the tiny object with a big pink tongue, and it was squeaking shrilly.

'It'll live,' said Ollie, as proud as if he'd arranged the whole business. 'Here's the next. See how fast they come?'

They stayed another hour, under the flickering light of a hurricane lamp, until the last came.

'Six,' said Ollie. 'That's the lot. See, she's starting to feed them now.' And the six small shapes, struggling strongly and clawing each other's faces with total ruthlessness, climbed across the wet hay between their mother's legs. There came a sound of tiny sucking, and at the same time a tiny purring, smaller than a distant bee makes on a summer's day. The old cat lay belly to belly with Lord Gort, making a warm, defensive ring. Both cats began to purr, but their pink tongues never stopped licking.

'God, I've lived to be nigh sixty-four and I've never seen that afore,' said Stevo in hushed and reverent tones. 'Ain't nature wonderful?'

'An' you owe me ten bob,' said Ollie, heartlessly. 'Let's go to the pub. Cats'll be fine now, wi'out your help.'

10

For the next two weeks, all went well. Lord Gort showed no ill-effects. Next day she was prowling and ratting again, leaving the kittens in the care of Skinny. Skinny was loving it, except when the kittens tried to feed from her withered nipples. Then she moved away just far enough. Lord Gort became a prodigious consumer of rats, and at first put on weight, till the demands of feeding the kittens began to drain her.

Skinny prospered, too, but mainly from the tremendous amount of kitchen-scraps delivered by Ollie and Stevo, who seemed to find cause to go into Trojan's stable a dozen times a day. They were old men; even their youngest horse was middle-aged. They had no children or grandchildren. The kittens were the first young life the stables had seen for many years.

At first the kittens' instinct kept them completely safe. When not feeding, they slept in a tight-packed mass for warmth. If the sudden arrival of Lord Gort or Skinny scattered them through the hay, they would crawl and roll, fall and claw, squeaking wildly until, almost by pure accident it seemed, they were back in their packed mass again. Until they were eleven days old, their eyes were closed, their ears were folded. They were blind and deaf and that kept them from wandering.

And then, on the fourteenth night, came tragedy. The biggest and boldest, a tom kitten, went wandering, got lost, and fell through the hay on to the floor. Lord Gort was out hunting, and Skinny, left in charge, was asleep after a wearing day in which the kittens' attempts to feed, and their sharpening claws, had been especially trying. The kitten squeaked in distress; but Skinny had heard so much squeaking, she did not awake.

The kitten, overcome by curiosity, began to half-walk, half-crawl towards the door, following its mother's latest scent. It passed the great hooves of Trojan, who was fortunately quiet in sleep also.

And then the rat came. Its first attack took the kitten by surprise; the kitten did not know the smell of rat. It took it for one of its own siblings, and pushed and bit in retaliation as best it could. Then the rat's teeth bit harder. The rat began to drag the kitten towards the stable door, still struggling. The kitten's squeals increased. It was a hard and bitter fight; it was a big kitten. In another week, the rat would not have dared.

Too late, Lord Gort came leaping home; too late, Skinny wakened and leapt down. Between them, the rat did not last two seconds.

But it was too late for the kitten . . .

Lord Gort sniffed it once, and turned away to the living. Skinny sniffed once and joined her. It is impossible to tell if they grieved. Soon, the manger above was again a purring mass of cats and feeding kittens.

Only Ollie and Stevo grieved. It was the first death.

*

101

The next Thursday, they were getting ready for a dance in the barn. They'd helped themselves to a couple of drinks from the brandy bottle Ollie kept for emergencies, to get themselves in party mood. Tonight, the barn would be fuller, the girls prettier, the band better at playing the good old tunes than ever.

Stevo was warbling monotonously, 'If you were the only girl in the world, and I was the only boy . . .'

'God help us, if you were the only boy,' said Ollie. 'You drunken old bugger.' But there was no spite in him. The old tunes brought back memories. That Sunday School picnic in the summer of 1901 when they'd all ridden out in the flower-decked carts to Coleshill and he'd first taken a smit to the missus . . . It had been different when the missus was alive. She'd made him get dressed up for church on Sunday mornings . . . shopping trips on the bus to Birmingham . . . summer holidays at Southport. The world, she'd made it a wider place. Now there was just the horses and work and making money for God knew what, and the pub every night. He hadn't been out of his working clothes since the war started.

It was at that point that Lord Gort started getting under their feet. Running backwards and forwards, ferreting into the deepest, darkest places; under the little stage for the band; behind the heavy cupboard where they stored the lemonade and ice cream soda; chirruping to herself urgently.

'What the hell's up wi' her?' asked Stevo.

'Mebbe she's peckish for a quick rat . . .'

Then Lord Gort disappeared, and re-appeared

102

again with a kitten held awkwardly drooping in her mouth.

She vanished under the stage with it; then emerged alone and ran off purposefully.

'Makin' a new nest,' said Ollie. 'They often move the kittens after a few weeks. When they start teachin' them to hunt.'

'She'll not find many rats under there tonight. More like empty bottles ... The band'll drive her crackers. And the kittens'll get under people's feet ...'

They stopped, suddenly worried, as the bewildered kitten emerged at a stagger from under the stage, and came towards them, mewing piteously.

Lord Gort returned, carrying another kitten, which she dropped at their feet, to pursue the first again. It squeaked with pain, as she bit it in her haste. She put it back under the stage, and ran off for another.

'She's gone flipping *crackers*,' said Stevo. 'What the hell are we goin' to do wi' her?'

They looked at each other uneasily, as if the cat had suddenly let madness into their cosy world. She had always been such a *wise* cat ...

She returned with a third kitten, just as the first re-emerged from under the stage. Now she ran wildly from one to the other, as they tottered in different directions, clawing at them, almost as if she were *fighting* them. Her ears were back, she ran low to the ground, kept changing her mind.

'She's bloody terrified,' said Stevo. 'What's she frightened *of*?'

'We'll lock her up,' said Ollie. 'Maybe she'll

quieten down. We can't have this, wi' the dance. You fetch the kittens.'

He picked her up. She was rigid for a second, like a cat made of metal rods, then she began to fight like a thing demented. Her claws raked Ollie's cheek, and in a rage he swore at her and hit her, a thing he'd never done to a cat in his life. The tension, the madness was spreading to him. She went limp, so he thought for a moment he'd killed her. Then she started fighting again. By the time he'd slammed the stable door on her and the kittens, he was bleeding in half a dozen places.

'*Blast* her. This shirt was clean on, for the dance. What do you think's . . .?'

'Listen,' said Stevo. 'It's the dogs . . .'

They stood and listened. The night was dark and very silent. But all through the crooked cobbled back-streets of Coventry, in the cluttered yards behind the timbered houses, the dogs were barking.

Then one, close by, began howling. Stevo shivered, and rubbed his bare arms. 'Never heard that afore . . . but that's what's upsetting her.'

'Why should dogs . . .?'

And then the sirens went. Stevo pulled out his old watch and squinted at it. 'Ten past seven. Jerry's early tonight. That's buggered up the dance.'

'It mightn't be much.' All Ollie felt was outrage that the dance might be spoilt.

But Stevo said, 'Don't like the sound of it. The sirens sound . . . different.'

'Tripe! Jerry'll be after Birmingham again.'

And then they heard the drumming of the planes.

'Jesus,' said Stevo. 'Hundreds. Old Hitler really means it tonight.'

And then the sky lit up. Far brighter than moonlight. Ollie felt, under that terrible light, like a fly on an operating table. Waiting to be swatted. He wanted to run, but there was nowhere to run to. The whole tiny crooked wooden city lay on the same operating table, under the same awful light that turned rooftops and chimneys and the spires of the churches into a brilliant black-and-white photograph.

'Flares,' said Stevo. 'They're dropping chandeliers.'

Ollie looked up. Whole new constellations hung above him, blinding out the stars. Some were near, some were far. They swayed in clumps and moved across each other silently, as the wind caught them. A few search-lights came on, but they looked weak and faded, puny and helpless, like the arms of a drowning man. The four guns behind the Hawker-Siddeley factory opened up, but what good could four do?

Ollie felt he was a fool for ever having felt happy, ever having looked forward to the dance. Please God, he thought wildly, please switch off this terrible light. *Please* give us our night back.

Ack-ack shells burst overhead, blinding stars that left a black starred hole in your eye afterwards. But they couldn't switch off the light or stop the mad drumming of the planes.

Then came a thin sighing in the sky, a fluttering in the ear. He pushed Stevo back into the stable doorway. 'Shrapnel.' Stevo, with his safe billet in Boulogne in 1918, would never have heard the sound of shrapnel falling.

105

But it wasn't shrapnel. They heard something rattle like a load of tin-cans being dumped. Far and near, loads of tin-cans being dumped on the tangled buildings of Coventry. A load landed on their own stable-roof. Two objects fell into the yard at their feet, and burst into fountains of blue sparks, giving off white smoke, like sparklers on Bonfire Night.

'Bloody thermite,' said Ollie. 'Bloody incendiary bombs.' He thought vaguely how pretty they looked. Then little yellow flames began to run up the wheel of a cart parked nearby.

'Get the hose.' Thank God the hose for hosing down the yard was still connected.

The hose was a mistake. Under its impact, the bomb rolled, sent off clouds of white smoke, and broke into a dozen leaping, burning pieces that landed everywhere. But in the end the weight of water was too much for it. They weren't much worried about the other one; it was burning itself out harmlessly, burying itself in a heap of very wet manure, sending off only a totally evil cloud of choking smoke.

Stevo raised his head. 'Christ, they're all over the roofs.'

'Get the ladder. I'm going up.' Ollie kicked off his floppy slippers and grabbed a hayfork. The round rungs of the ladder bit into his bare feet, but he hardly noticed. He shouted, 'I'll knock 'em off and you spray 'em. But steady wi' the water.' He was glad his feet were bare; they gripped the rough slates, making him feel sure of his footing.

Most of the sparkling bombs were lodged in the gutters. He went along flicking them neatly into the yard with the fork, shouting warnings as he did so. Once they were on the stone cobbles, they couldn't do much harm. Only . . . there was one that had cracked its way through a slate, and wedged itself at the bottom of the chimney . . . it came out suddenly, as he gave a frantic upward heave with the fork. He fell over backwards and rolled down the roof, and only a last-minute grab at the top of the lavatory pipe saved him from a nasty fall into the yard. His fork, suddenly released, fell like a spear, missing Stevo by inches.

But that was the last of the bombs. He lay watching Stevo deal with them; poking them contemptuously into the middle of the yard with a stick, making a harmless bonfire of them.

'If that's the best Hitler can do,' Stevo shouted up, 'he might as well have stayed at home.'

Then the guns opened up again, as more bombers came over. Ollie got off the roof quick; he knew what shrapnel could do. He went and got his old tin hat, from Caporetto days. The chin-strap was as hard and sharp as a bit of bent tin, but it was better than nothing. Stevo produced an old bowler hat from somewhere, and stuffed it with newspaper.

There came again that same rustling in the air; that same tin-can rattle on the roof . . .

But the second time it was easier. He knew his way around the roof now; his flicks with the fork were more expert. Afterwards, they spent some time settling the horses, who were growing restive. In Trojan's stable, they noticed that the two cats were coiled in their defensive ring round the kittens.

Then the third lot came down. One went through

the roof into a hayloft, but Stevo got the hose to it straight away. Nothing to it, he said casually.

But up on the roof, Ollie had seen a change coming. There were big fires now, on three sides of them. And his bare feet were no longer cold; there was a breeze that was warm, like a spring night. Everyone had not been as lucky with the bombs as they had. The night was full of the bells of fire-engines. Only, the fire-engines did not seem to be coping. The distant fires got bigger; the air got warmer. Summer heat now. And the fires on the north and east seemed to be joining up . . .

Stevo called out, 'Pressure's gone from the hosepipe!'

Something old and wise moved in Ollie's mind; something also very sad. He called down quietly, 'I think we better get the horses in the carts. I think we might have to pull out.'

'We can *manage*,' shouted Stevo, defiantly. 'We don't need the water. We can put them out wi' wet horse-shit.'

'Aye,' said Ollie. 'Mebbe we can manage, but there's others that can't.' There came a scorching Saharan gust of air that scared him; he came down off the roof, out of the heat and the light. It was still cool and dark in the inner shadow of the yard.

They had to work in the dark; the chimneys of the house, now glowing orange, gave them only a little light. But they were horsemen of fifty years' experience. The smooth worn leather, the thin brass buckles moved sweetly under their hands. Soon they had horses between the shafts of all seven carts. Luckily, one cart was still full of sacks of corn; the horses wouldn't go hungry, however long they were away. Then spare harness went into another cart.

Stevo went upstairs and packed two suitcases with clothes as best he could. They stripped the blankets off the beds, put aboard the battery radio and the two old rocking-chairs. There was the sound of many feet running on the cobbles outside; people yelling at one another, sounding frantic. There were air-raid wardens among them, too, blowing whistles.

'Time to go,' shouted Ollie. He looked down. Lord Gort was standing there, a kitten dangling limply from her mouth. 'Damn me, we almost forgot the kittens.'

Stevo ran and fetched them, and stowed them safe among the blankets of the last cart. Old Skinny lay on top of them, panting with heat or terror, her eyes like slits against the terrible glow in the sky. But Lord Gort still ran to and fro, across the cobbles, as frantic as if one kitten were still lost; though Stevo had carefully counted five.

Ollie swung open the great doors. The blast of heat and light that streamed in terrified him. The air seemed to suck the moisture out of his old lungs. He saw the grocer's shop across the road, the one on the corner, was burning, its glass gone, and fringes of flame licking out round the wooden door-frame. They'd have to pass that corner.

He reached up for Sampson's bridle. And Sampson, the pride of his heart, Sampson the leader, Sampson who feared no lorry, refused to move. He shied, and began to back away from the gates, making his cart twist and bang into the next cart. Ollie thought it was all up; there was no time to get all the horses

109

blindfolded, which was the only other way, and that mightn't work.

Then Lord Gort stepped forward tentatively. And then, very unhappily, she walked through the gate. And down the street. And, marvellously, Trojan stepped after her. Ollie dropped Sampson's bridle, and grabbed Trojan's instead. Looking back, he saw horse after horse following Trojan, the carts rumbling into life. They were on their way.

11

They all got safely past the first corner, though the flames reached out through the shop window like giant searing hands. Beyond, they plunged into a canyon of shadowed dark. The temperature dropped so suddenly that Ollie shivered. But at the far end of the alley, a red light glowed like the sun. And from the heart of that sun, shouting. They began to tread on fat coils of white hosepipe, that peed upwards in weak little fountains, soaking Ollie's legs. It was the most beautiful cooling thing he had ever felt. But the effect was only for a moment. The air got hotter again, as they pressed on towards the red light. Between jets, his trousers steamed and dried.

He took a deep breath and led Trojan out into the light.

There was a cliff of flame, four storeys high. He couldn't even recognize what building it had been. But beyond was something he could recognize all too well. The cathedral was a black cage of flame. The fire raged to break out like a caged tiger, shooting out great paws of sparks through its bars, reaching for anything that might be within reach. And yet, oddly, as they shouldered their way past it, heads down, there seemed to be the sound of dripping running water inside. There seemed to be little silvery streams running out between the old tombstones to their very feet. Streams that halted for a moment; went dull and grey. Then cracked open to release more shining silver streams. Trojan shied as they tried to step over the first; a wave of heat came up. Ollie saw.

They were not streams of water; they were streams of molten lead. From the roof. They learnt to step high, after that.

In front of St Mary's police station, firemen were gathered with hoses. Water still came out of the hoses, but without force. The white jets did not even reach the cathedral; they spilled weakly onto the steaming pavements. 'No pressure,' cried the first fireman he came to. 'We can't get no pressure. The roof-girders is white hot. They're pulling the pillars apart like Samson . . .'

Even as Ollie looked, the chancel roof fell in. The tiger reared up into the heavens, trying to claw at the spire, which still stood; leapt out towards Ollie, too, in showers of sparks, coals of burning wood; a burning blizzard that stung like claws. Trojan began to twist and jibe, as the hot coals bit into his smooth back with a dreadful stink.

'Do us a favour, mate. Dowse the horses down, afore the sparks drive them mad. Dowse the carts, dowse me.'

Obediently, the fireman turned his hose. He looked like one of those negro automatons in fairgrounds, with his black face and pink lips and white eyes and teeth. But his hose did the job thoroughly; it was like bathing in a mountain stream, full of force and life. A draught of cold air seemed to come out of the hose as well, sweet as champagne. Suddenly and deliciously shivering, Ollie passed on.

'Keep heading that way, mate,' shouted the firemen. 'It's the only way still open.'

It was a meaningless maze of fire and dark. But still the cat led on. Strange smells, like Christmas. Roasting beef, from the cold-storage warehouse; smoking cigars from the burning tobacconists. A body lay in their path, a giant, dull grey, and vilely twisted. But Trojan did not shy; he walked straight by it. Only then did Ollie realize that it was the statue of Peeping Tom, blown from its pedestal. Beyond, they had to ford a warm stream of rich-smelling melted butter.

Jerry was dropping high-explosive now. You couldn't hear the explosions above the steady rumble of the flames, but you could feel the cobbles rock under your feet, and then a spark-blizzard would come roaring down the narrow funnel of the street, and you had to shut your mouth and stop breathing.

On they went, past a big fire engine, trapped by falling walls and on fire itself; past a fireman being led along between two others, his face like a cooked steak and his pale eyes unseeing, rolling wildly in all directions.

At last a cool breeze set into their faces; a breeze that seemed to Ollie to promise open fields and woods and mossy places. They burst out of the narrow world of burning timber, into the modern world of concrete factories and wide-open spaces . . .

And the air-raid was still going on. Searchlights still tried to pierce the red rolling clouds of smoke, so low overhead. A few guns still banged.

As he watched, bemused, a bomb struck an office-block at the gate of a distant factory. The building seemed to expand like a balloon blown up at a party, like a house in a cartoon-film. Then all the glass windows blew out, and the building settled back into itself with a rumble of falling bricks and slates, and became no more than a hole in the ground.

A frantic warden ran up to him. 'Take cover, take cover!'

'Where's the bloody shelters for horses, then?' shouted Ollie, suddenly so mad he could've hit him. But the man wasn't listening. He was only another brainless marionette, who ran down the line of horses shouting to them 'Take cover; take cover!' and leaving a vicious whiff of sweat and urine behind him.

Blindly Ollie walked on behind the cat, his shoulders hunched as if he were walking through teeming rain. His neck ached from the weight of the bobbing tin hat and from the impulse to pull his head right inside his body, as if he were a tortoise. The only thing was to walk out of town, to where there were no guns or bombs or fire, but only bare winter trees and bleached winter grass and peace. He no longer looked behind to see if they were following; the rumble of iron wheels and the clop of hooves were enough; he could hear, far behind, Stevo grumbling soothingly at the horses.

He looked up only once; as they were passing the Morris engine works. The long sheds were roofless now, and windowless; the ragged brickwork mocked him. Jerry had done for the new Coventry as well as the old. Wardens and rescue-men were scrambling inside, with the brainless wandering of ants whose nest has been destroyed.

At last there came a moment when the sudden stillness penetrated his brain. Such a silence that he stopped, wondering if he were dead. But it was only that the raid had stopped; the guns were silent; no more bombers flew overhead. He walked back down the line of carts, counted seven as they closed up behind him and stopped in turn. Saw the drooping weary familiar heads: Trojan and Sampson, Willie and Emperor, Duke and Duchess and Marjorie. And, tied to the tail of the last cart, Benjamin and Sarah. In the dim light of the distant fires he saw the dried foam round their mouths, the tiny burns and wounds from the cinders that made them look spotted like leopards. Singed, half-beat, but safe.

Stevo looked at his watch. 'Twenty past six. The longest night I've ever known. I never thowt to see the sun again . . .'

'Sun's not bloody up yet,' said Ollie. 'Don't count your chickens, you drunken old bugger.'

'Naw, we done it,' grinned Stevo, out of a face as black as any fireman's. 'We'll dance on Hitler's grave yet.'

'Where's your false teeth?'

'Back in the house. I took them out for comfort . . .'

'I wouldn't recommend nipping back for them . . .'

Together, they looked back. Beyond the broken, empty-windowed factories, there was nothing but burning. Only the three spires of the churches leant above the flames, like spoons set in a soup of fire that was a living thing, a red beast that waxed and waned, that seemed to breathe, drawing in the cool air of the countryside past their stinging faces and burning eyes. Ollie's eyes watered so much he didn't know whether he was going blind or just crying.

'Coventry's finished,' said Stevo.

'Aye,' said Ollie, 'but we're not.'

He glanced round to get his bearings. There was a signpost, but it had no pointing fingers. The Home Guard had taken them away, to confuse German paratroopers. But he recognized a group of cottages. Suddenly he stopped being a terrified crawling tortoise and became a haulage contractor again. He had some very shocked and weary horses to look after.

They began to overtake people. Mothers dragging crying children along. Men with bundles of bedding on their shoulders, or in prams. At first, the groups parted when they heard the rumble of the carts and Ollie's warning shouts; parted without looking back, without looking up. They seemed oddly familiar; Ollie thought he had seen them before somewhere. But where? In a dream? Then it came to him. In the newsreels at the cinema. In Holland, France and Belgium. Refugees, fleeing.

Good God, he thought. It's happening here, in England. Hitler's doing it in England now. And his heart suddenly froze with fear.

Then a man stepped out into the road. 'Give us a lift, mate? We can't carry the kids any further.' He was a well-dressed, well-spoken man, in a collar and tie, trilby hat and raincoat. A man used to giving orders, but he was pleading now, humble as a beggar.

116

Ollie looked around; a crowd of similar figures had gathered from nowhere.

He said, 'The kids can have a ride. The rest of you will have to go on walking.'

The man seemed to change in a moment. He walked down the line of horses, shouting, 'Kids can have a ride. The rest of you will have to walk,' with real authority in his voice. People obeyed him. Kids were lifted up. Little rows of dirty faces stared down from the carts, their thumbs in their mouths, silent.

Then the man came back, obedient as a soldier, and reported, 'All the kids are aboard. Where are you heading for?'

Off the top of his head, Ollie said, 'We'll make for Coleshill.' He didn't know why he said that except the kids piled on the carts made him think of the Sunday School outing, all those years ago, when he'd first taken a smit to his missus. Coleshill would be an awkward place to get to, from here. But all down the line of wagons, he heard voices crying out gladly, 'We're going to Coleshill; we're heading for Coleshill; we'll be all right in Coleshill, Coleshill, Coleshill, Coleshill.' As if there were something magic in the name; as if Coleshill was the Promised Land, and he was Moses, leading the Children of Israel. Or, he thought, looking back at Coventry, as if I were Lot, leaving Sodom and Gomorrah, the Cities of the Plain.

Well, he thought, I've said Coleshill, so Coleshill it shall be. He took good old Trojan's head-collar, and turned the cart to the left at the next crossroads. He felt better himself, to be going somewhere definite.

In that strange bleak winter dawn, he saw two things

he never thought to see. Even though he was drunk with strangeness, drugged with it, so they seemed like things happening in a sleepwalking dream.

First a huntsman, bright in his hunting pink, sitting in the middle of the road astride a great dappled grey horse. The man's face was clean, and pink, too, with fresh shaving. His hunting boots shone like black diamonds. Without saying a word, he held up his whip, signalling them to stop. He seemed to Ollie a man of infinite authority . . .

And when they had all stopped, the hunt came streaming across the road. The well-groomed eager dogs, running nose to ground. The gentlemen and ladies calling and laughing softly to each other in spotless red and black and the ladies with white stocks at their throats. Not one of them looked at the carts or the people in them.

They crossed, and vanished like a dream; the huntsman turned his horse and galloped after them.

Don't they *know*? thought Ollie. Don't they *care*? What do they think we are? Gypsies?

The other thing he met was a woman carrying a pie, walking towards Coventry. A fine, juicy home-made pie that had slopped gravy down her coat. She was only wearing carpet slippers, but she looked weary, as if she'd walked a long way.

'Have you come from Coventry?' she said. 'Have you seen my husband? He's a fireman in the AFS. Called Pykett. He went to Coventry. He hasn't had his tea yet.' She glanced down at the pie.

At the sight of the pie, Ollie's stomach gave a great gush of juices. But all he said was, 'How far you walked, missus?'

118

'From Hinckley . . . ten miles.'

'He'll enjoy that pie, missus,' said Ollie gently, 'when you find him.'

She limped on, gravy still dripping on to her coat.

In the bleak November morning, it began to drizzle. A cold wind got up. He was worried about the horses; they weren't country horses, used to standing out in the fields all night. They were used to a warm stable, and two square meals a day, and plenty of fresh water. He looked at Trojan; the old horse looked fit to drop, with new foam round his mouth. If I don't get them under shelter soon, I'll lose them, he thought. And he hadn't brought them out of the fiery furnace to lose them now . . .

And then he looked at the people following behind, and was ashamed at worrying about the horses. The children lay huddled in heaps on the carts; asleep, they looked horribly like little corpses. He was compelled to look closely to make sure they were still breathing. The adults, heads down, were just putting one foot in front of the other. He thought, with a surge of panic, there must be hundreds of them. What was he going to do with all these people? All he could do was to keep on walking towards Coleshill, and keep his eyes open.

The first interesting thing he saw was a half-ploughed field; a field being ploughed for winter wheat. But a tractor was stuck in the middle; something must have happened to its back axle, the wheels were at ridiculous angles to one another. He noted it, and passed on. Down into a little valley, with a stone bridge over a clear little stream. Then a short but steep hill, up which poor old Trojan slipped and laboured. The horses must be damn near finished . . .

And then he saw the farm: a big old farm, with plenty of stabling and a big barn. Dare he ask at it? No smoke came from the chimneys. The farmer should be up and about by this time; the farmer's wife should have the fire going for his breakfast. He hovered . . .

Lord Gort leapt down from the first cart, and headed up the track to the farm at a trot. God knew what was in her head. Probably she was just hungry and wanted a rat . . .

But she drew him after her . . .

The farm track was overgrown with weeds. The farm garden a wilderness. There were long dead strands of grass growing up through the cobbles of the farmyard, like pale ghosts. Two of the farmhouse windows were broken, with dirty rags of curtains blowing through. Ollie knocked on the back door, hope suddenly blooming in his heart . . .

No answer. He looked through a window into the kitchen. No furniture, except a big table and two chairs tossed over on their backs. Abandoned.

He walked round the silent wet farmyard. Stabling for twenty horses; they must've bred horses here once . . . Still plenty of hay showing through the round holes in the lofts.

A sudden rumble behind made him spin round. Trojan sniffing the stable smell, sniffing the promise of hay, had followed his nose, and turned into the farm track. And behind came the other horses, the carts, the children, the people. Things were going too fast for Ollie's poor tired mind. Suddenly the farmyard was full of people looking at him, with hope dawning on their hopeless faces. The rain began to fall even more heavily. Children, wakened by it, began to cry.

Ollie decided to do the first illegal thing in his blameless life, apart from fiddling the Income Tax.

'Right,' he shouted. 'Get under cover. You can sleep in the haylofts.'

Children were being lifted down stiffly. The man in the raincoat came up with three or four men behind him. 'What do you want us to do?'

'Can you get into the farmhouse? Get a fire going. Fetch some water. We'll try and brew some tea . . .'

A new voice cut through the air. 'What the hell are you lot doing in my farm?'

He was a very ugly customer, with three days' growth of beard on his face, and a loaded shotgun in his hands; hands that trembled with rage, and pointed the gun straight at Ollie's belly.

12

Ollie told himself he must keep calm. It wasn't very difficult; he was too tired to be anything *but* calm. He didn't believe that any of this was really happening; except he had a tingling in his belly where the lead shot would hit him if the farmer pulled the trigger.

'We've come from Coventry,' he said, looking over his shoulder to where the vast smoke from the burning city ascended to the grey clouds and vanished into them. 'Coventry's finished. Gone.'

'I couldn't care less,' said the farmer. 'Get off my bloody farm!'

'You're not using it,' said Ollie. 'This farm's not been used for *months*.'

'I *own* it. I don't want these bloody riff-raff crawling all over it.'

'They've got nowhere else to go. There's kids. They're soaked.'

'Let the bloody government look after them. They started the war . . .'

'But . . .'

'Get off my farm!'

The people watched, with white, hopeless faces. The kids began to cry louder. Women began to cry, too, helplessly, awfully. Worse, Ollie could hear the men murmuring.

'He's trying to throw us off!'

'Knock the bastard on the head!'

Several men began to edge forward. They were dressed like ordinary working men. But their faces were strained and desperate. Ollie had a growing feeling that somebody was going to get killed.

'I'll pay you rent for the place,' he shouted. 'Four quid a week . . .'

As he said it, he remembered that all his money was stuffed inside the mattress of his bed back in burning Coventry. He'd never trusted banks. He'd avoided paying income tax. Well, it was all gone now. All he had was the twenty quid of dealing money in his jacket pocket. He suddenly felt like crying.

'Twenty quid,' shouted the farmer, a cunning look drifting over his face. 'Twenty quid a week and a month in advance. Or get off my land . . .'

Ollie held up his hands in a helpless gesture. The white-faced men from Coventry edged a little nearer. One said, 'Twenty quid a week? That's four men's wages . . .'

'He's a racketeer. Fill him in!'

The wailing of the women and children drove them on. Ollie had never heard a ghastly sound like it, except the noise the Italian women had made in 1918, when one of their men was killed. These are *Britishers*, he thought, desperately . . .

There was a loud honking of a motor-horn, on and on. The ring of people parted, slowly, dazedly, and an army truck drove through. There was an officer driving, with a policeman sitting beside him. Four soldiers with tin helmets and rifles jumped out of the back. Ollie wondered, in a dream, why they had their bayonets *fixed*. Were they *expecting* trouble? There was a thin, clerkish man with them, with a bald head, spectacles, a little moustache and a very expensive overcoat that for some reason had mud all down one side.

'Who's in charge here?' shouted the officer. He was far too excited; there was sweat on his upper lip. He had a revolver at his hip and the flap of the holster was undone.

Ollie said quickly, 'I am.' He was amazed at himself. He'd never had charge of anything but horses all his life. He'd only been a private at Caporetto . . .

'Right,' said the officer. 'What's your name?' Then he turned to the thin man with the moustache. 'Write his name down!' He turned back to Ollie. 'What's the name of this place?'

'Tall Trees Farm, Coleshill,' said the farmer, trying to get back into the act. That was a mistake. The officer and, even more, the policeman looked at the pointed shotgun trembling in his hands. The farmer, realizing things were turning against him, lowered the gun quickly. But it was too late.

'Who is this fool?' asked the officer.

'He's trying to chuck us out,' said Ollie. 'The farm's been empty for years, but he's trying to chuck us out. These bairns will die of cold.'

'It's my farm,' said the farmer stubbornly.

'It *was* your farm,' said the officer with dislike in his voice. 'It's now been requisitioned by the government as an official rest-centre.' He turned to the

124

clerkish man. 'Give him an emergency requisition order.'

'What about my rent?'

The officer waved a hand in his face. 'Talk to the city council. When there is a city council again. If ever.' He turned to Ollie. 'We'll get what help to you we can. Try and make a list of everybody you've got here, will you? Right?'

And they all got back in the truck and drove away.

Ollie turned to the farmer, spitefully, 'I'll give you two quid a week rent . . .'

'You said four before!'

'That was *before*,' said Ollie. He held out eight quid from his wallet. 'That's for a month. That's more than you'll get off anybody else. And you'll sign this receipt . . .'

He pulled his old receipt-book out of his pocket, and his old indelible pencil, and made the farmer sign.

Ollie went into the farm kitchen, pulled one of the overturned chairs upright, and sat down at the table. He stayed there for the next six hours, clinging to the table in the sea of chaos that followed, like a shipwrecked sailor to a raft.

Stevo and the man in the raincoat came to see him; they were white-faced, arguing.

'All the people are in the stables,' said Stevo. 'I can't get the horses in.'

'People are more important than horses,' said the man in the raincoat.

'Look,' said Ollie patiently. 'It was the horses that got you here. It'll be those same horses that will fetch

125

the food in for you. If they're sick from getting wet, they can't *work*.'

The man in the raincoat nodded. He had sense, that one. He said, 'I'll talk to them,' and went off. Half an hour later, the horses were eating hay in their stables.

The pair of them came back.

Stevo said, 'The people are pissing and shitting all over the place. There'll be nowhere to walk and sleep soon.'

'Find some shovels,' said Ollie, wearily. 'Dig some trenches in the farmhouse garden. There's a pile of old newspapers in that cupboard. One to each family . . . Tell them to go canny with it. There's not an endless supply . . .'

The man in the raincoat went. Ollie was getting a great respect for him; the other men listened to him. He must be a foreman from one of the works.

Ollie turned to Stevo. 'I wish I had some bloody money. Them kids'll be starving . . .'

Stevo turned to an old suitcase lying in the corner. Ollie thought it was one of those they'd packed with their clothes. It had a familiar look . . . Stevo dumped it on the table and clicked it open with a flourish.

It was full of banknotes.

'Where the hell . . .?'

'Didn't you know I knew your secret hiding place in the mattress?' grinned Stevo. 'You stupid old bastard. I've known it for years. Helped meself to many a quid on a Saturday night. How'd you *think* I could afford to buy you all those drinks? Did you think I was Carnegie?'

Ollie swore at him horribly; then thrust his hands

126

deep into the banknotes he thought he'd lost for ever. A wave of thankfulness swept over him; they were going to be all right.

Slowly things came together. Other useful men came in, asking what they ought to do. Someone found an old bicycle and was elected messenger. Stevo got Sampson back into a cart after six hours' rest, and went off round the farms with a wad of notes that would've choked a horse, looking for something to eat. The man in the raincoat, who was indeed a foreman from the Daimler works, went round the people coaxing them into giving up what they'd brought to eat. An incredible mixture. Half-packets of biscuits, tins of soup, tins of condensed milk, half loaves of bread. A woman turned up who said she was a cook. All she had to cook with was two old battered galvanised buckets, and one of them leaked. In the end, all she could do was concoct some horrible kind of soup, everything mixed in with water and boiled. But enough for the kids.

Stevo returned with only three dozen eggs and two sacks of potatoes, and they cooked them in the buckets, once the kids had had the horrible soup. Stevo said that now darkness was falling again, the roads were alive with refugees, frightened of another raid.

Many of them turned up at the farm, and quarrelled over sleeping spaces with those already there. Stevo said there were so many in the hay-lofts, he was frightened the rafters would collapse. People were putting down blankets in the mud of the old pigsties; people were sleeping in the farmyard itself, even though it was starting to rain again.

No one came to help from the outside. Soon after dark, the sirens sounded again over ruined Coventry. Ollie went out for a breath of fresh air, and watched the living, pulsing glow of the fires four miles to the south.

Then the German bombers came back. Ollie stood knee-deep in the sleeping people of the farmyard, watching the flashes of the first bombs in the sky. Some of the people moaned in their sleep, but they didn't waken. Old grannies, tiny kids, slowly getting soaked by the fine rain. Ollie knew there'd be real illness if help didn't come by morning ... There were three hundred and twenty-six people on the man in the raincoat's list. Three hundred and twenty-six people left in *his* care. Oh, Moses, he thought. How did *you* do it?

Then he thought bitterly: God smote the rock for Moses, and clean water flowed out. God sent manna in the wilderness ... where the hell was God *now*?

His only comfort was that the horses were all right; only old Trojan was coughing a bit, making the little kids who slept packed round his great hooves stir uneasily ...

And the cats and kittens were all right. Lord Gort had gone straight to an open drawer in the cupboard by the fireplace. Steadily she had carried in her kittens from the cart, one by one. She must still have kept her milk – a miracle after what she'd been through; the kittens had suckled and were comfortably asleep, stretching as the warmth of the cooking-fire, fuelled with broken fence-rails, reached them. Lord Gort looked up at him smugly, pausing in her washing of the kittens.

'It's all right for some,' he said.

Lord Gort blinked at him blandly, and turned to washing Skinny.

13

They had a committee meeting of sorts the following morning. All the blokes who seemed to know what they were doing, mainly foremen from the various works. And the three women who had volunteered as cooks. Except, as they said, they had nothing to cook.

'I've been going round since first light,' yelled Stevo. 'The farmers won't even talk to you now. They're all waving shotguns. There's refugees everywhere, pinching turnips and spuds from the fields. Wringin' hens' necks and stealin' sheep. One lot even tried cutting a cow's throat . . .'

'What about Coventry?' Ollie asked the bloke with the bike wearily. He got the same old reply.

'Coventry's finished. The whole town centre's flat. All the shops is gone. Even in the suburbs the shops is empty. Everybody's getting out. Just the firemen left, and soldiers lookin' for looters. And nutcases wandering about babbling to theirselves. I got out afore I was shot. The fires is still burning, worse than ever. Fire brigade's just given up . . .'

'All right,' said Ollie, sharply. The man was getting hysterical.

'What'll we give the bairns to eat?' asked one of the women, in the silence that followed.

'We could slaughter one of the horses . . .' somebody said from the back.

'Over my dead body,' said Ollie. Then wished he hadn't said that. A vision of himself dead seemed disturbingly clear and real this morning, as the silence resumed.

Then one of the men said, 'There's a van coming . . .'

They all ran outside.

It was a large van. A clean, shining van. With *Herbert Moore, Baker* emblazoned in large letters on the side. There was a soldier with a fixed bayonet alongside the driver, who wore a white coat and a desperate expression.

But from the inside of the van came a smell that made their mouths water.

Within seconds, everyone at the farm was round it in a deep ring.

Two soldiers jumped from the back, holding the doors wide. And there was the overwhelming smell of fresh-baked bread.

'Get in a queue,' shouted the soldiers. 'Get in a *queue*!'

Slowly, shuffling, a queue formed.

'Mothers of families. One loaf each.'

Ollie never forgot the forest of hands reaching for bread. The soldiers' hands giving it out; filthy hands tearing up the gleaming golden loaves in great chunks, stuffing bread into the holes in filthy faces.

The queue broke. There was just the forest of clutching hands round the back of the van. The soldiers stopped shouting; one got his steel helmet knocked off by the reaching hands. The rule of

131

'mothers of families, one loaf' just vanished. Hands reached, old hands, little hands, brawny hands, mud-caked hands, and the soldiers fed the hands blindly, sweating, scared.

Ollie was terrified the loaves would give out. But still they came and came and came. Slowly the forest of hands diminished, until everyone was wandering around and sitting on walls, a loaf under their arm, tearing great chunks off it.

'Want a loaf, mate?' called out a soldier to him. 'It's the last.' The loaf sailed wildly through the air, and landed in the mud at Ollie's feet. He picked it up, and his hands, too, began to tear at the crispy crust, as if they had a life of their own. He stuffed bread into his mouth until it was a great, wet, unmanageable wodge that he had to chew and chew and chew on. Still chewing, he watched the empty van drive away, bucking over the ruts in the farm track.

But at least nobody had got hurt, thank God. The people wandered off, clutching the remnants of their loaves, dazed, docile.

And at least the sane outside world still existed. Somebody cared. But Ollie wondered who was going to pay the sweating baker for the bread.

It was never so bad again. The food arrived in jerks, but it came. One day they all lived on bully-beef; the next all on baked beans. The day after that, con-densed milk, bread and eggs. The fourth day, seven WVS women set up their mobile kitchen, and Ollie no longer had to worry about food. But nobody could wash; there was only enough water and

132

buckets for drinking and cooking. And the trenches dug in the farmhouse garden stank to high heaven.

From the hungry time, it became the cold time and the smelly time. And the time for grief. Men walked into Coventry, to try to talk to the wardens, what was left of them. To search the wards at the Coventry and Warwickshire Hospital or Gulson Road for those who were alive but had forgotten their own names. To walk shuddering into church halls doubling as mortuaries . . . and to return home with stiff white faces.

Ollie tried to comfort where he could. People were very odd. He found one woman in hysterics, and spent two hours trying to comfort her before she managed to get out that her mother was alive, only with a broken leg. Whereas those who'd lost somebody moved round quietly, often being helpful. And then there was the dreadful evening after they buried 420 people in a mass grave in Coventry, because nobody could tell who they had been . . .

And yet things got easier for Ollie. The number of people at the farm began to drop, as people found somewhere with friends and relations and moved out. On the Friday, the man in the raincoat, whose name Ollie finally discovered was Fred Street, reported there were less than two hundred people left and everybody had a dry roof over their heads and hay to lie on and plenty of bedding. A supply of coal for the farmhouse kitchen range finally arrived, so they could stop burning fences.

But everyone still said Coventry was finished. That was the day Ollie borrowed the old bike and went to look for himself.

As he passed the dead Morris engine works, he wondered if it were truly dead. The car park was full of cars and lorries. Inside, through the broken windows, he could see men moving about in over-coats and sou'westers, in the rain that fell through where the roof had been. Rubble had been piled in great heaps outside. He asked the man at the gate, and the man said that, though the whole roof had gone, the lathes and presses were all right. Maybe there could be an open-air factory. 'Be nice, next summer,' he added, drily.

A bit encouraged, Ollie cycled on, trying to find his stables. The streets had been cleared by a new sort of tractor with a big shovel in front. They were still at it. Somebody said they were called 'Bull-dozers'. Ollie stood and watched one of them working; like a great green dinosaur eating the rubble with shining jaws.

But, though the streets were cleared, they only ran through still-smouldering piles of cinders and rubble. Ollie would never have found the pile that had been his stables, if the metal street sign hadn't been left lying loose on top of it.

Aye, well, he thought, I was right to get out when I did. But it was a cold comfort, when he was homeless.

The one thing left standing was the spire of the cathedral amidst the blackened cage that had been the nave. He walked in, appalled. He hadn't been inside a church since he'd buried the missus, but he was sorry it was gone.

Somebody had nailed two long, thin, charred roof-beams together to make a cross, and leaned it against

134

the remains of the altar. Behind the altar itself, some body had chalked:

FATHER FORGIVE

Ollie did not feel at all like forgiving. He cycled past cats and dogs, sitting at garden gates, waiting patiently for their owners, outside houses that had vanished for ever. A kitten playing in the garden of a bombed house, leaping at flurries of charred paper as they flew past in the wind like flocks of birds, while the blanket-wrapped corpse of its owner was carried away on a stretcher . . . Who was going to feed them all – care for them?

He got home feeling empty, hopeless, and sat at his old chair at his old table, and put his head in his hands.

There came a bright chirrup. He looked up, and there was Lord Gort, standing on her hind legs, her paws on his thigh, offering him a fresh dead rat. Her eyes were bright; her fur groomed and immaculate; not a hair out of place. In the drawer, her well-fed kittens slept with Skinny. Her whole world was in order, and now she was offering him help with his . . .

He leapt to his feet, shamed.

'By God,' he roared, 'if a cat can do it, so can I!' He paced up and down, suddenly hot for action, but not knowing what action to take. If only he had some place to call his own, like she had . . .

And then he remembered the men scrambling inside the Morris factory. The suburbs, windowless, roofless, but still standing.

Something went click in his mind. There was still

135

life in Coventry, outside the dead centre. If it revived, all the people at the farm would go home some day. Their numbers had already dropped a bit . . . maybe two families could live in one house . . .

Mind made up, he cycled to the farmhouse where the farmer lived who'd threatened him with the shotgun on the first day.

He was threatened with the shotgun again, till the farmer saw who he was. Then he was asked in. Even offered an enamel mug of tea with some whisky in it.

He sensed something was up.

'Fancy selling a couple of your horses?' asked the farmer, a bit too casually.

Ollie remembered the broken tractor he'd seen on that first grey morning. It was still there, stuck in the middle of the field, useless. And nobody would be coming out of bombed Coventry to mend it, not for a long time. And the man would be wanting to get on with his ploughing for the winter wheat. He was badly behindhand . . .

'I don't sell horses,' he said. 'But I hire them. Four quid a day for my best pair.'

'Two,' said the farmer.

'Three,' said Ollie.

'Two pounds ten.'

'On condition you sell me the farm buildings I'm livin' in.'

The farmer glared at him suspiciously, from under black eyebrows. 'What you wanta buy them for? They're requisitioned. They'll be a government rest-centre for the rest of the war. Them refugees is pulling everything to bits. There won't be nowt left worth having by then . . . Coventry's finished.'

'I like to own where I live,' said Ollie, stubbornly. 'I don't like to be beholden to a landlord. Four hundred quid for the buildings, and the paddock next door.'

'Seven fifty,' said the farmer, a knowing, cunning glint in his eye.

'Five,' said Ollie. 'And not a penny more.' He slid some notes from his wallet on to the table.

'Six.' The farmer's little piggy eyes followed the fall of notes greedily.

'Five fifty,' said Ollie.

'You're bloody mad,' said the farmer, exultantly.

Ollie worded the receipt very carefully, as his own father had taught him. Then he cycled back to his new home, looked at Lord Gort sitting in her drawer and said, 'You in your small corner, and I in mine.'

Lord Gort looked at him with shining orbs, rocking and purring as if she approved totally. He thought she understood every word he said, just like a little Christian.

The farm changed hands formally four weeks later.

By that time, less than twenty refugees remained. And there were two old cottages to house them in. Empty, the farm would be worth two thousand pounds.

Father Forgive, thought Ollie, as he cycled away from the final signing.

But business was business.

14

Slowly, life joined up, as people found each other again. Five of Ollie's old carters drifted in, one after the other. He learnt sadly that Tommy Pierce and Harry Higgins had died in the bombing. But there was plenty of work for carters in the city centre. They all worked from dawn till dusk, often finding their way back to the farm exhausted, in pitch darkness. Rotten work, though. The debris they carted was full of reminders; half-burnt family photographs, broken toys, little dresses. Once, a dreadful thing they thought was a shrivelled wax doll, till a passing Heavy Rescue man took it away wrapped reverently in a torn tablecloth. But there were useful things as well: pots and pans; once, miraculously, an unbroken mirror. Ollie comforted himself that no one knew who they belonged to; they were on their way to the tip, anyway.

There were bargains, too. People who'd been bombed-out wanting to sell their furniture. Ollie gave fair secondhand prices, and refurnished his house and cottages with lovely old stuff. And one day he saw three big horses he thought he knew, shivering and wretched, every rib in their bodies showing through their unloved, wet, shaggy coats. They were on a handkerchief of green grass they'd cropped down to the roots. They'd be dead in another fortnight. He traced Joe Smith's widow with a lot of difficulty. She said he could have the horses for nowt, if he looked after them; she hadn't given them a thought since Joe died in the bombing. He pressed fifty quid into her hand and ran away from her grief.

In that desperate stricken city, everything Ollie touched turned to gold. He had the room to store things, and the ready notes to buy them. Best of all, he had the cat to talk things over with, before he made his decision. She just sat and purred; didn't say daft things back, like Stevo. She was like a wife to him.

He grew fat on other people's misfortunes, and it bothered him. He had a haulage business twice its old size, and a grand big house fully furnished, and he was a landowner for the first time in his life. Maybe the paddock was only four acres, but it gave the horses a taste of green grass and somewhere to roll and frolic.

His guilty conscience made him tender with other people. The day the last of the refugees went to an official rest-centre, Fred Street came to him, and asked to have one of the cottages to rent, permanently.

'I'll do it up, Ollie. Couple of my mates will help. Only I don't want the missus and kids going back to Coventry. The factories are working again – Jerry'll be back any day now.'

Word got around. He rented out the other cottage, too. And the top floor of his house. Not only did his old suitcase start to fill up with notes again; there was also company he liked. Kids playing; young wives gossiping in his kitchen. One little lad began calling him 'Granda' and soon they all, adults as well, began referring to him as 'Granda Burton'. As he strove to be fair and keep the peace among them all, again he felt a bit like Moses, the patriarch of a very large tribe. For years, his life had been closing in; now it opened up endlessly. He was asked to sit on committees. He spent all his unused clothing coupons on a new suit.

The cats prospered, too, after some early wheezing. Skinny, now as fat as butter, seldom stirred from the drawer. But Lord Gort was the queen of his kingdom; went everywhere about the place with him. Stevo might grumble about the rats' heads and tails left everywhere, but in Ollie's eyes she could do no wrong. He had a deep feeling she had brought him all his luck.

Ollie did the rounds of his families on New Year's Eve, 1940, with a large bottle of whisky in his pocket from a source best not asked about. The families were not short of New Year cheer themselves.

And when he finally got back, Stevo said, 'You old soak, you're as pissed as a newt.'

'Aye, mebbe so. But I'll give you a toast, Stevo.' He poured two tumblerfuls, with a not very steady hand.

'Damnation to Hitler in 1941!'

'May he rot in hell!'

'An' another toast! Prosperity to us. We'll make enough money this year to go to Berchtesgaden for a week, and dance on Hitler's grave every day.'

'We'll stay for a month an' dance on his grave every day!'

The two old men leaned forward in their rocking-chairs and embraced each other round the shoulders. '*Every* bloody day.'

'And get drunk. Jerry's gotta drink called schnapps – it'll blow your bloody head off, Stevo. An' them nightclubs in Berlin – girls in black tights an' top hats an' not much else. Oooh, we'll have a time after the war – we'll have to get passports . . .'

'An' dance on the bugger's grave for a whole bloody year!'

Suddenly, Ollie, sobering up, got, wobbling, to his feet.

'Another toast, Stevo! The cat! That led us out o' the Land of Egypt!'

'God bless her!'

Lord Gort seemed to realize she was approved of. She blinked at them three times; then turned modestly away to blink into the roaring fire that burnt only wood these days, wood from destroyed Coventry.

One morning, a month later, she wasn't there at breakfast time. And one of the kittens, the biggest, was missing with her. Old Ollie didn't work that day, he wandered the fields calling with increasing hopelessness; she was his luck and he felt his luck had run out on him. He asked in every place he went, for weeks afterwards. But there was never any word of her, or the kitten. He had his carters check the roadside verges for black bodies, but they reported nothing.

He comforted himself that she had left four off-spring as black as herself, to carry the luck on.

And then the blizzards came, and he lost himself in new problems.

*

It is not certain why the biggest kitten followed Lord Gort. Perhaps he was the only one awake when she slipped out. Perhaps he thought he was following her on a hunt; she had begun to take the kittens out hunting, in ones and twos. And he was a tom, the most bold and enterprising.

But she was on the hunt for more than rats that morning. Her person had suddenly reappeared to the north east, and not so very far away. She set off at a steady, mile-consuming trot, which the kitten found very difficult to keep up with. He was long in the leg now, but very short on stamina. Often she got so far ahead, her very scent grew faint. His heart would fail him, and he would cower, beaten and terrified, under some bush.

But some vestige of mother love remained in her. After he had called and called in his distress, she would come back for him, clout him angrily for his weakness, then feed him and urge him eastward again. It was more than her person's presence that made her impatient; she could smell, feel on the moist tip of her nose, the terrible cold approaching from the east.

Mrs Wensley opened Geoffrey's letter, surprised it was post-marked 'Louth, Lincolnshire' and not 'Winnipeg, Manitoba'.

My dearest Flo,

Sorry to amaze you like this, but I couldn't tell you we were coming – the censor would have had it in the waste-basket before you could say 'Adolf'. I'm posting this in a civvy postbox in Louth, so it should get to you without being disembowelled.

Well, as you can see, we're back in Blighty. I think they got a bit tired of me preaching the vices of Blenheims and they're giving me a new toy – a Vickers Wellington or Wimpey for short. From what I hear on the bush telegraph, Wimpeys are not only bigger and faster, but incredibly tough and hard to write off. They have a lot of guns in all the right places (where the squirrel keeps its nuts) and, best of all, they fly by night when all the little Messerschmitts are tucked up safely in bed. They even issue them with return tickets!

Even better, I have the chance of a furnished house. It's just across the airfield, but well clear of the flight-path, so you won't have your ears pulped all day by passing Wimpeys. It looks a bit drear and draughty under snow, but there's a big wild garden yearning to feel the touch of your hand, with a flowering cherry to park young Jeff under in the spring, and plenty of lawn for him to crawl on. And I've found a woman in the village who could help you with the housework.

We can afford this, because in their muddle-headed way they've given me a squadron to look after, and made me up to the grand rank of acting wing-commander. Let me assure you that you will be getting the very model of a modern wing-commander – the Mark Ten version with supercharger. I have put on a stone, with all that Canadian hospitality. I'm as brown as a berry from the prairie sun, and the old hand has long since stopped shaking, so I can hold even my eighth pink gin without disgracing myself.

On the other hand, if you can't face it, I shall quite understand. I can live quite comfortably in the mess. I know what a pain-in-the-arse I was on my last leave. I don't think I'll ever be such a pain-in-the-arse again, but if I ever am, I shall make a noise like a hoop and simply roll away.

Let me know what you think. Give young Jeff a hug from me . . .

She packed with a sinking heart. He was cheerful, but he was not Geoffrey. He was chatting her up as he might chat up a blonde popsy in the mess.

15

Susan Marriot came up out of a lovely warm sleep, and immediately tried to get back down into it again, before memory came back. A bit like a U-boat forced to the surface trying to dive again, before more bombs hit it.

She did not succeed. The memories came flooding in, and she was wide awake. Timothy was dead. Timothy was gone. The house was empty. Even if she went up into his workroom, he would not be there. How often she had tiptoed up to that work-room, scenting the smells of balsa wood and engine-oil and fabric-dope, opened the door and expected him to look up and grin at her. She had done it even after the telegram came; done it *more* after the telegram came. As if by creeping up and opening his workroom door, suddenly, she could summon him back from the bottom of the sea by an act of magic.

He was so much *there* in that room. The half-built model ship still lay exactly where he had placed it. He had picked it up, looked at it, put it down *so* and taken her in his arms for the last time. She could still feel the shape of his arms across her back. Every tool in its place, where he had left it. His old shabby coat with the drooping pockets still hanging on the back of the door. A packet of Player's Navy Cut, with nine fags still left inside; a Swan Vestas box with five live matches and two dead ones.

Dead ones. Nobody knew how Timothy had died; his ship had simply vanished without trace, crossing the Atlantic. Six months ago. Since then, in her writer's mind, Timothy had died a hundred different deaths. Blown to pieces by a torpedo in the engine-room, never knowing what killed him. That was the best death. But it was too easy, too much a comfort. She had rejected it. Instead, he desperately tried to escape up the engine-room ladder, knocked back again and again by the cascading water. Or he went to the bottom of the sea, still alive, trapped in an air-pocket with his hands beating vainly on the metal door jammed against him. Or he floated face upward, disembowelled by the explosion, while the gulls ate his intestines and perched on his face and picked his blue eyes out. Or he died in fire . . .

She lay, staring upwards at the light-fitting, letting the images of Timothy's death pour through her mind unchecked. She felt dead, floating herself, unable to move hand or foot. She often lay in bed for hours, unable to move.

The neighbours had been very kind. She hated the kindness of the neighbours more than anything; the false voices they put on. The false cheerfulness that grated; the false sorrow that grated even worse. How could *they* be sorry, when they had husbands to go home to?

She had tried to carry on her life as usual; doing things because she had always done them. She had managed very well for the first month, while there was still some vestige of hope. Everyone had told her

146

she was wonderful. Grinning like a skull, she trod the treadmill. Washing on Monday, ironing on Tuesday, shopping in Oakham on Wednesday. She had even finished the novel she was writing when she first heard his ship was missing. It was inside her, like a child, and insisted on being born. She had sent it off, and her publisher had praised it highly. But the praise did not reach her heart, did not light a glow where a glow should have been. And after that, nothing else had been born in her that wanted to see the light. Inside, she was hollow, dark, empty.

Then, there seemed no need to shop; why should she strain to seem cheerful, pleasant to people? Afterwards it left her exhausted. Why should she exhaust herself to comfort other people, spreading the lie of her own cheerfulness? Timothy had seen to it, before he left, that she had a larder full of tinned stuff.

So she stayed home. And then it suddenly seemed foolish to bother to get dressed in the morning. Why *should* she bother, if she wasn't going out? So she stayed in her dressing-gown. And why bother to cook? It was suddenly impossible to cook for one, though she had always managed it before when Timothy had been away at sea.

And why do the washing, when there were no clothes needing washing?

She drew back the curtains in the morning with reluctance. If it was a grey day, it made her feel worse, as if there were other grey curtains beyond the ones she drew. If it was sunny, it was a cruel mockery, as if God himself had already forgotten Timothy's death, and decided to be happy again.

Her only moment of savage joy was when she drew

the curtains for the night. Lock the door, lock the uncaring world out and huddle over the log fire for warmth, snug as a child in the womb.

Until the thoughts of Timothy's death descended, homing in on her mind like vultures . . . Sometimes the phone rang. She took a vicious delight in not answering it, in listening until the fool gave up hope. That would teach them what it was like to give up hope . . .

She suddenly became aware of something scratching at the bedroom window. What could it be? she wondered idly. One of the bushes in the garden blowing in the wind? But she listened, and she couldn't hear any wind.

The scratching came again; it annoyed her. Every time another daydream of Timothy dying came, the scratching came as well. The world wouldn't even let you be miserable in peace. The fourth time it came, she leapt out of bed in a rage, and pulled back the curtains. Ready to shout her head off at anybody who was there.

There was nobody there. But for a moment the view took her breath away. The Vale of Catmose lay under an enormous blanket of snow, feet thick, that must have fallen in the night. All the field walls and fences were buried. The hedges and bare trees looked like Christmas puddings, dusted with sugar. And from a vivid blue sky the sun shone, making the snow glint, acre on acre. From her isolated hilltop, she could just see the tower of Oakham church beyond the white blanket, miles away.

For a moment, she was five years old again, clean, innocent and happy. And then she thought with bitter glee that the snow was a shroud, come to bury her. It was alarmingly deep; she was cut off from the world. No bundle of false cheerfulness could come knocking at the door; even the postman could not get through with his brown sheaf of problems. She was truly buried at last.

In a mood of grim satisfaction, she threw on a jumble of clothes to keep warm, including a pair of Timothy's thick mountaineering socks, and went through to the kitchen to revive the fire and make a mug of tea. She took the same grim satisfaction in re-using a dirty mug from the heap of undone washing-up; of simply adding to the mound of tea-leaves in the unrinsed teapot. The tea came out hot, but bitter as gall; well, that suited her. Life was bitter as gall. She spooned in condensed milk and two sugars. She was getting in a bad way, and she didn't care.

Suddenly, the scratching came again, at the kitchen window. She turned, and there was a black cat on the windowsill. It saw her watching, and miaowed a silent appeal to be let in. An arrogant appeal, she thought. A case of: 'You *can't* let this happen to me. Life's not *like* this. I have the right to *live*.'

Little do you know, chum, she thought, little do you know.

A sharp gust of wind suddenly hurled itself at the house, howling in the chimney and sending smoke out into the room. It drove a flurry of deeply frozen snow into the cat's black fur. The cat flinched, turned on this new enemy, eyes slitted.

You're learning, chum, she thought, you're

learning. Turned her back and tended to the reviving fire.

After five minutes, she looked again. The cat was still there: again, it miaowed desperately. She knew it was not one of the village cats; she knew them all. She had been quite fond of cats before Timothy died, though she'd never kept one. It must be a stray. Well, it could stray off somewhere else . . .

The cat gave one last despairing miaow, and leapt from the windowsill as the flurries of snow grew more intense. Immediately, perversely, she hurried to the window to see where it had gone.

It was leaping in strangely vertical leaps towards the wood-shed. Every time it landed in the snow, the snow came up to its belly. The snow was too deep for it to cope with really. It wouldn't be able to go far till the snow melted.

Then she saw another black cat follow it. Well, not a cat, a half-grown kitten. The kitten couldn't cope with the snow at all. It floundered after its mother with terrible struggles. She hadn't felt sorry for the cat, but she couldn't help a twinge of pity for the kitten. Then she forced the pity out of her mind. With men dying at sea at this very moment, dying in the freezing water, who had pity to spare for a kitten? It should thank God it was at least on dry land . . .

Later, the snow began to fall again, fast and thick, whirling out of nowhere and piling up against the window-sashes so she could hardly see out. God, it must be cold out there. She imagined Timothy's mangled body floating, covered with a grim new flesh of ice that gathered on his bones until he was an iceman, a snowman . . . God, suppose he came to land and walked home to this cottage, and one morning there was a snowman in the garden, all jolly, and then when the thaw came, the snow melted and revealed . . .

But her mind would not hold the image. It went back to that black kitten, floundering through the snow. It would be inside the wood-shed now, shivering, starving. She felt great pity for it; tears flooded swiftly into her eyes. But she made no attempt to open the door and help it. It would die soon. Well, it would die anyway, in the end; even if she helped it, fed it, it would grow old and die; even if it avoided illness or being run over by a motor-car, it would die in the end. Everything died in the end. She herself would die in the end . . .

She came to with a start and realized that the fire was burning low, and that there were no logs left in the hearth. She would have to go out and get some. Oh, hell. She hauled on her muddy wellingtons, got a sack and opened the door.

The snow had stopped again. The sun shone, the world glistened, the cold fresh breeze played round her face. A tiny traitorous pleasure crept into her mind, a purely animal pleasure at being. She stamped on it quickly. There could be no pleasure in a world where Timothy was dead. She trudged heavily through the deep snow to the woodshed, slamming down her feet with every step, as if to crush to pieces the tiny pleasure she had felt.

As she thought, cat and kitten were huddled together in the furthest, darkest corner. Again, the adult cat miaowed, though less certain of itself now. She ignored it, and began to pile logs into the sack.

151

When she had enough, she looked again to where the cats were crouched.

The bigger cat was gone; must have run away terrified. The kitten watched her with big hopeful eyes, trembling. It swallowed nervously. Its mouth made a very dry sort of noise. She realized it must be thirsty . . .

Well, get on with it, chum. She hefted the bag of logs, and waded back through the snow. She was nearly at her door when she saw the new cat foot-prints in the porch. The back door was swinging gently open. The big cat was in the house.

Indeed, it was crouched low on the littered kitchen table, hurriedly eating the rind from the plate of bacon and eggs she'd cooked herself three days ago; her last cooked meal, if you didn't count baked beans eaten out of the tin with a spoon.

She opened the back door wide, and advanced on the cat. It watched her warily, but didn't move; went on licking the congealed egg from the greasy plate avidly. She suddenly grew afraid; it was a big cat, and plainly desperate. It was not afraid of her; it might leap at her face. She ran to the corner of the kitchen and grabbed a broom. Made a swing at it. The cat dodged the broom at the last moment; the broom hit the plate and broke it in half.

'Damn you! *Damn* you!' She chased it round the kitchen, flailing with the broom.

The cat ran upstairs. Ran under the bed in her own bedroom. She shoved the broom under the bed and flailed it about vigorously. The cat emerged like a rocket, ran out on to the landing and leapt on top of the blanket cupboard.

Beside herself with rage, she flung the broom at it. The broom-head missed and hit the little trap door that led to the cock-loft in the roof. It leapt from its seating, leaving a dark gaping hole in the ceiling. She recovered the broom and jabbed at the cat again. It snarled, clawed at the broom, but she forced it to one end of the blanket cupboard. She'd have it in a minute . . .

Too late she saw it gather itself for another leap. Next second, it had vanished through the trap-door into the loft.

She sat on the stairs and wept; she felt so hopeless and exhausted. She should get a ladder and get up there. But the loft was pitch-dark and full of old suitcases and junk. Up there, the cat would see better than her; move faster than her. She might put a foot wrong and fall through the ceiling.

Finally, she walked away and left it. Hunger, and the smell of food from the kitchen would bring it down in the end. She'd better cook herself something that smelt good for lunch . . .

But she got to the kitchen and just sat, staring at the piles of washing-up in a daze. Suddenly shocked by how weak she was. The way the battle with the cat had exhausted her. Before Timothy died, she had often walked twenty miles a day and never felt tired, as her mind roved free seeking new ideas for her books. She hadn't realized her body could go down-hill so quickly. She was still *young*; only twenty-eight. Had she developed some dreadful invisible disease that could kill her in weeks? She imagined her own death, alone in the bedroom upstairs. If she died, who would find her body? The milkman, the postman?

153

Or would they send for the police to break in? How would she look, lying there? A dead object, an object of revulsion they would talk about in the village for weeks. Would *The Times* carry an obit? 'Death of promising young author'? What would they say of her? 'Tragic waste of a brilliant talent'?

By dusk, she had still done nothing. The fire had burnt down again, and all the morning's supply of logs was gone. She would have to go out for more soon; it was starting to get really dark. There was still no sign of the cat from upstairs. It must have had a good feed from the wreckage of the kitchen table, and gone to sleep up there. Not giving a damn about its kitten, out in the cold . . . Animals were cruel, heartless. Like the rest of creation. She dreaded facing the kitten in the darkness of the log-shed. It might be dead by now, cold, stiff.

But the fire burnt down and down; the kitchen got colder and colder. In the end, she had to go.

In the semi-darkness, the kitten was just a black blob, unmoving. Was it dead? She couldn't hear it breathing. She didn't like to touch it, but somehow she had to know.

It felt very cold. But just as she was thinking it was dead, it mewed under her hand, giving her a terrible fright. It moved, feebly, and again swallowed, as if it were very thirsty. Then it hunched down and seemed to go to sleep again.

She hesitated; then picked up the bag of logs and went back into the house. Made up the dying fire. Tried to think of Timothy, but thoughts of the kitten kept getting in the way. She would have to face it again, when she went for logs in the morning. By

154

then, it might be dead. How would she bury it, with all the snow on the ground? But she couldn't leave it in the corner, to greet her as a decaying corpse every time she went for logs. An eyeless corpse . . .

That thought drove her out of the kitchen and down the garden like a rocket. She fell twice in the snow, she was in such a hurry. When she finally reached the shed it was so dark she couldn't see the kitten. She had to grope for it. When her hand touched it, it felt even colder; but again it stirred, mewed, swallowed drily. It was shivering. She shoved it inside her coat, and blundered her way back into the house. Slammed and bolted the door, as if all the devils in hell were after her.

She made up the fire into a real furnace. Got a cardboard box, put an old towel in, and set the kitten in it, by the hearth, so the hot coals wouldn't fall on it. It stayed hunched up in a tight ball. When she felt it half an hour later, it didn't feel much warmer, or much more alive. Though the room by that time was *roasting*. She became convinced it was going to die. In a panic, she picked it up and pushed it inside her coat, next to her body. Its coldness seemed to enter her own heart, through the wool of her jumper. It would die, it would die . . .

Exhausted, she fell asleep.

She was awakened by a wet nose pushing against her cheek. The kitten had its eyes open. It mewed, asking for something. She heated some milk in a pan, tested it carefully with a finger, and set it down on the table, and put the kitten to it.

The kitten sniffed it dubiously; turned away. Then turned back and began feebly to try to lap. She held

155

it closer, helping it by putting milk on its mouth with her fingers. Finally, it drank properly. She had won. It wasn't going to die.

In her moment of triumph, she looked up. The mother cat was standing in the doorway watching her. After a moment it trotted across the floor warily, jumped on the table and finished up the rest of the warm milk. Only then did it walk over to the kitten and start to lick it. It looked at Susan, with an expression of triumph on its face, as if it knew it had won. Finally it called the kitten over to the box by the fire, and they settled down together, purring.

Weary, totally defeated but somehow triumphant, Susan opened a tin of best corned beef and gave it to them. The mother cat ate wolfishly; the kitten half-heartedly, with many pauses. If Susan hadn't inter-fered, the kitten would hardly have got any.

Susan suddenly realized she had no idea what time it was. The clock on the mantelpiece had been stopped for days; it was pitch-black outside the snow-plastered windows. She had to turn on the radio to get the time. She was amazed that it was ten o'clock. She banked up the fire with nutty slack and staggered up to bed. She had not given Timothy a thought for *hours*. She tried to think of him now, but the thoughts would not come. And in an instant she was asleep.

By lunchtime the next day, Susan had come to the conclusion the cats were a damn nuisance. As soon as the snow had melted, she'd get the RSPCA to come and take them away. It was the big cat who was the bother. She kept on foraging for food in the wreckage of unwashed plates and cups on the kitchen table. Susan had to wash up everything and put it away before she got any peace. Then she found both cats settled in the wreckage of her unmade bed. Frightened of fleas, she made her bed for the first time in weeks. But it was mainly their constant *hunger* . . . They never stopped asking for food. She couldn't afford to go on opening tins of expensive rationed corned beef. And there was no more milk for them; the milkman hadn't been able to get his horse and cart up through the drifts from the village.

She'd have to go down to the shops. She'd have to get dressed properly. She'd have to get washed. It seemed to take her ages. Her clothes were stuffed into the wardrobe any old how, all creased to hell. She had to sort them out, get out the ironing-board. *Damn* the cats. Her best skirt was too tight at the waistband; she got it fastened but it nearly cut her in half.

But when she stepped out into the brilliant sunlight, washed and dressed, she felt *different* somehow. Businesslike, with her purse and ration book; but nervous suddenly of people. Still, nervousness would not feed those damned cats . . .

The first person she passed was Mr Addinsell, briskly shovelling snow from his drive; eighty years of age, flushed and thoroughly enjoying himself. She took a strange slight pleasure in looking at his wire-rimmed spectacles and rosy cheeks. Mr Addinsell greeted her with a flood of news about the snow. Who had been cut off; who was digging out their sheep. He seemed to have forgotten who she was, that she was a tragically bereaved widow. He was much too interested in the difficulties of the snow ploughs over Melton way. They chatted amiably for ten minutes, then he went back to his shovelling. Walking away, she realized he had not given her a single pitying glance.

Further down, by the school, she fell on her backside in a snowdrift, and got snow in her knickers. It made her feel oddly . . . young. A complete stranger, a young farmhand, picked her up and dusted her down with heavy hands. His eyes and cheeks, too, were bright with the adventure of the snow. She blundered into the butcher's and everybody turned and said hello, and listened avidly to her story of her fall, and about the two strange cats who had suddenly appeared on her doorstep.

The butcher looked at her ration book, baffled. She hadn't drawn her meat ration for nearly a month. She could have anything she liked. He had some nice pork chops. And plenty of lights for the cats, certainly. Be sure to boil them well for half an hour!

She struggled back up the hill, puffing dreadfully. But halfway up she realized that something had changed in her. She had left a cosy timeless land where she lived alone with dead Timothy and, think as hard as she might, she could not get back into it. A door had slammed behind her. Oh, Tim dead was real. The loneliness and emptiness were real. But no more real than old Mr Addinsell, and the butcher. Why should she shut *them* out? To pretend they didn't exist was *absurd*. Of course they existed.

16

The mother cat remained wary, though she came quickly enough for her share of the boiled lights. She hadn't forgotten or forgiven Susan's attack with the broom. But the kitten came to Susan with complete trust, settling on her knee by the fire at every opportunity. It even tried to come to bed with her at night. That moved Susan to tears. She had meant to let the kitten freeze to death, and yet it loved her. She felt like a condemned criminal suddenly released from the dock. She felt absurdly rescued, grateful.

So the next morning, when she heard the kitten sneeze, and saw it wipe its nose with a paw, she felt a sudden and unreasoning fear. If it took ill and died, she would still be condemned.

She told herself she was worrying about nothing. Made up the fire and set the kitten by it, in its box. But it went on sneezing all the morning, all hunched and woebegone. Still, it ate some lunch, without much enthusiasm. She'd heard that as long as they went on eating and drinking, they would be all right, even if they did have cat flu. She left an extra-full saucer of milk by it.

At tea-time, it refused to eat. She felt its nose; it was hot and rough. She was sure that was a bad sign. She rang the vet; the vet didn't answer. She peered out of the window; snow was starting to fall again. She had never felt so desperately cut off from the world in her life.

At eight, the vet finally answered. He was curt. He sounded tired to death. She told him the symptoms. He tried to choke her off. Then his voice changed; he'd remembered who she was, remembered she was the tragically bereaved widow.

He said, 'I'll be in the surgery for the next half hour. If you can get him down here . . .'

She rang off in triumph; suddenly, being a widow had its uses. Outside, the snow was still falling, but not heavily. She needed something to carry the kitten in. It might escape from her shopping basket . . .

Basket . . . Timothy's old fishing basket would do. She walked into his workroom briskly, and grabbed down the basket from the top of the cupboard. For the first time, she entered as if the room were not a church, not a holy of holies. She had no feeling that Timothy might be sitting there, smiling at her. She never thought about it. She wanted a basket; that was all.

She lined the basket carefully with an old blanket and put the kitten in. Then she set off briskly, with the basket banging against her hip, from the leather strap over her shoulder. Pushing through the whirling flakes excited her, as it had when she was a child. She made the surgery in twenty-five minutes. The light was still on, showing through the blackout curtain.

She held the kitten, while the vet poked a thermometer up its backside. 'It's gotta temperature,' said the vet, abruptly. He groped under its chin, behind its ribs, rather roughly. The kitten tried to escape;

160

she crooned to it, and gentled its ears, and the kitten was still again. 'Glands are up,' said the vet. 'I'll give it something and you can have some tablets – two a day, morning and evening.'

'Will it . . . live?'

He looked at her. He was not a handsome man, or young. His grey hair was clipped as short as a convict's, and he'd shaved badly that morning – there were patches of grey stubble under his nostrils where the razor had missed. 'He's got as much chance as you or me. Kittens are tough little sods.'

She remembered the vet's wife had died last year, of cancer; after a long illness, as they said. Yet here he was, rushed off his feet. She wondered if he was going home to a cold house . . .

'Can you do me a favour?' he said. 'Can you feed this lot?' He indicated a small row of cages which seemed to contain two dogs, two cats and a rabbit. 'Otherwise they're not going to get fed tonight. My girl's away sick – her damned husband's got her pregnant again. I've got a calving at Netherby Brow. I ask you, a calving at this time of year. I'll be lucky to be home by morning . . . the grub's all there, ready-mixed. Put the light off and hang the key on the rail in the porch when you go. There's a good girl . . .'

'But . . .'

'Go on; it won't take you five minutes. You're good with animals . . .'

And then he was backing his car out of the piled-up slush in the yard and was gone.

She managed to work out what the animals should have from the three bowls. Bran mash for the rabbit, and a few bits of old cabbage. Evil-smelling fish for the cats, and evil-smelling meat for the dogs. It all seemed rather old and stale. But the animals wolfed it down, as if they hadn't eaten for days, while she stood watching with a strange feeling of ownership. Their cages could do with cleaning out; the whole room could do with dusting. She was sorry for the vet, that his wife was dead and his girl sick, yet she liked being in the surgery. It was like being allowed to wander through someone else's life: the reading spectacles on the desk; the picture postcards from before the war pinned to the wall. The heavy black rubber waterproof hung behind the door. It was gently interesting to drift through life as a spectator ... Painless.

After half an hour, she picked up the kitten in its basket, put out the light, locked the inner door and hung up the key ...

The blizzard hit her full force as she emerged. It snatched the air from her lungs, filled her eyes with snow and drove her back against the wall. It scared her silly. Then she took a deep breath, and strode out through the gate. She must not be silly and imaginative; blizzards couldn't kill you. This was *England*! Twenty yards up the road the blizzard knocked her clean into the hedge, and all the snow on the hedge fell down the back of her neck and into her wellies.

After that, she grew wary, walked hunched-up like a boxer, a soldier; braced herself for the wind coming viciously through the gaps in the hedge where the gates were. Even so, it had her reeling round the road like a drunk. The road had been cleared earlier by a snow plough, but the snow was grainy and deeply frozen; the blizzard picked it up and was piling it into new drifts, which sent showers down her wellies. First her feet seemed to be splashing in freezing soup, and then they went numb; it was like walking on the stumps of her ankles.

She fell more and more often; twice she dropped the basket in snow-drifts. When she tried to pick it up, her fingers inside her gloves were numb, too, like wooden clothespegs she couldn't feel.

She wondered desperately if she should turn back to the village, ask someone for shelter. But it seemed so *ridiculous* and, besides, she'd almost reached the signpost for the turn-off to Maltby House. She was just over halfway home.

She plodded; she staggered; at times she crawled on her hands and knees. She talked to herself; she talked to the kitten, though it didn't reply. And all the while, the wind searched through her clothes, up her skirt, at the gap between skirt and jumper under her coat, like an icy rapist reaching for her inner being. She remembered bitterly how often in the last six months she had lain in bed and flirted with the idea of death. Seen death as a gentle seducer.

Death was a rapist! She kept on muttering defiance. She did not want to die; she did not want the kitten to die. No, no, no, no, no.

Until she came to the four-foot drift that stretched across the whole road. She could never wade through *that*! She despaired, looked ahead for the last time, to say goodbye . . .

Her house was only fifty yards away; she could see the dim black outline of the chimney of the gable-end; the chimney was still smoking.

'*C'mon*, kitten!' She fought the snow with arms as well as legs. She swam through the drift, feeling the snow piling through her coat and skirt against her belly.

Then she staggered out on to a bit of road completely clear of snow, with even the white line up the middle showing. The wind, behind her now, carried her to the garden gate in a staggering run. She got through the front door, and slammed it shut against the cold and the dark.

She might never have been gone; the fire still burnt brightly; the mother cat, stretched before it, gave a silent, querulous miaow, wanting food. There was her favourite chair, her book, the reading-light throwing down a mellow glow. All hers; never so much hers as now. What we have we hold, she told herself with grim satisfaction. Death, try to take it away if you can!

But the kitten? She opened the basket-straps with fingers still clumsy from pins-and-needles. There was snow inside the basket, but only a very little. The kitten got up, stretched, yawned, jumped out and made hopefully for the food saucers. It licked at the few smears of gravy remaining. Reckless with joy, Susan opened another tin of corned beef for it. It ate quite a bit.

Susan went and changed. Made herself a cup of cocoa and sat and roasted her legs by the fire, and watched the cat wash the kitten.

Death, she thought, was always there in the world. In plenty. Always hungry, always probing for more. But it was *outside* now. Not in the house any more. Only a fool would invite it back in. She blessed

164

Timothy for his care of her; for the fire; for the logs he'd piled in the wood-shed on his last leave; for the stacked tins in the larder. Thank you, Tim, wherever you are. God bless you, for your love.

And just for a second he seemed to be in her mind, like a tiny bright spark. She knew without doubt that he was dead, but she equally knew without doubt that he still existed, somewhere, and was pleased with her. Then, while she was still understanding the spark, the spark was gone, and she knew somehow it would never return. But it was enough, to last her through all the nights and days to come. It would be ungracious to ask for more.

She slept in her chair, head back, mouth open, snoring gently. The cat slept; the kitten slept. Outside, the blizzard howled on, helpless to hurt.

The next day she rang the vet to tell him the kitten was better. Still wobbly, but eating. She asked the vet whether there was anything she could do to help while his girl was sick.

He asked if she could come in part-time, to clean and feed the animals, and help with surgery. For a pound a week.

With author's cheques for three hundred pounds on her desk, she gladly took the job.

Two weeks later, when the last snow was gone, the mother cat vanished. Susan thought at first, in terror, that the kitten had gone, too. But it hadn't; it was playing in the wood-shed and came to her, purring. But she never saw the mother cat again. On the other hand, she wasn't much bothered; the mother cat had never taken to her.

The kitten stayed, to grow enormous and live long.

It had learnt its lesson. It knew a good fire and an ample food supply when it saw one. It made a point of posing with Susan and her typewriter for the photographs that decorated the backs of her increasingly successful books. Thus, after the war, it achieved a certain fame, too. Susan was often tempted to call it 'Tim'; but that would be to tempt fate and death, and risk clever cracks from her literary friends. So it was never called anything but 'Kitten'. Which, considering its size, everyone thought very witty.

Meanwhile, Lord Gort pressed on. She felt she was very close to her person now.

17

It was the most trivial act of war that changed the whole nature of Lord Gort's journey. A German nuisance raid up the east coast towards Hull. Five bombers spaced at hourly intervals to keep the illusion of a real raid going as long as possible. To keep the inhabitants of Hull and Grimsby and Immingham sleepless in their shelters, so that they would go to their work in the morning weary and half-hearted.

The Germans did not even bring into use X-gerat, their radio-direction beam, to guide the bombers in. Consequently, the fourth in the stream got lost in cloud with a faulty compass, and drifted across Lincolnshire.

There, purely by chance, it was picked up by an equally lost RAF night-fighter, and shot at. It jettisoned its bombs in a panic – a string of eight 250-pounders – across the western edge of one of those small, forgotten Lincolnshire towns no traveller ever willingly passes through; a town of dusty brown terraces and yellow-brick chapels.

The first four bombs fell in the fields, which were given over to potatoes and turnips. A potato-clamp was hit. The area was well-covered with fresh vegetables the following morning, free to anyone who could pick them up. Most were gone by lunchtime, the loot of small boys excused morning school because of the raid.

The next two bombs fell in a little public park, splintering the trees and creating two new ponds when the craters filled up with water next day. It was a typical Lincolnshire January and the ground was waterlogged.

The eighth bomb sliced a little yellow-brick chapel nearly in half; one half was gone, the other kept its roof, pulpit and pews.

The only casualties were roosting rooks and wood-pigeons. The bomber escaped with half a rudder shot away; but since it was a Dornier 17 with twin-rudders, it lived to bomb another day. The night-fighter returned to base and made a 'doubtful' report.

The bomb that caused all the trouble did not explode. It made a typical small round deep hole in the only road leading into town. The local air-raid wardens, who had never had a real raid before, were *thrilled* to discover it. They blocked off the road with barriers and yellow UXB notices, and sent for the bomb-disposal unit. The local drivers had a long diversion round the side roads, but also had the joy of telling all their friends and neighbours about the UXB.

Well underground, the bomb ticked on. The bomb-disposal squad put it last on their list. It was causing no threat to life, and not impeding the war effort. When they finally arrived, a handful of locals gathered to watch from a distance. But after a few hours they drifted away; it was damp and bitterly cold, and all they could see were three khaki-clad figures enlarging the hole.

When Lord Gort came trotting down the road, it was nearly dusk. A satisfactory approach had been dug to the bomb, and two soldiers were down the hole working on it. There was another soldier hanging around on the road itself. His duties were to warn off any civilians foolish enough to pass the UXB signs, and to fetch tools from the lorry as required. Neither duty was arduous. He was eating a late lunch: corned-beef sandwiches.

Lord Gort smelt a trace of the sandwiches from beyond the barrier. She was hungry as usual. She was so near to her person now, less than ten miles away, and the feel of him was very strong. So strong, she had not bothered to stop and hunt for food. She lifted back her head and sniffed strongly, her nostrils working like a rabbit's. The smell was irresistible; she trotted under the barriers. UXB notices meant nothing to her.

The smell of human fear did. The bomb-disposal men stank of old stale fear. Their overalls were thick with it; their tools held the grease of frightened hands.

But the smell of bully-beef was stronger. Lord Gort approached the man and the hole.

'I should get away if I were you, puss!' said the man. 'If you value your life.' He was fond of cats.

But the cat didn't understand a word; though she caught the friendliness of the voice. She came nearer; almost to the man's feet, within a yard of the hole. The man felt he ought to shoo her away, be violent and abusive with her, for her own good. No kindness to her, if she went up in tiny bloody morsels for the birds to eat off the trees and telegraph wires. But he

169

knew if he chased her away she would only return, and this late in the afternoon his legs always ached with the day's tension, even though he'd done nothing but hang about getting cold. And he was bored, with nothing but the bomb to think about. She was a welcome diversion. So he threw her a lump of his sandwich.

He kept on throwing her bits; she seemed awfully hungry, poor sod, and he was chronically tired of bully-beef. When he stroked her, her spine knobbles were too sticking-out. That worried him, so slowly he fed her the rest of his sandwiches, stroking her while she ate gratefully, and saying things to her she couldn't possibly understand.

He was pleased when he got a purr out of her.

Then one of his mates down the hole said, 'You got a woman up there, Billy? If you can bear to stop crooning sweet nothings for a minute, go and fetch us another big wrench. We've nearly got this bastard; just one of the usual . . .'

But as he spoke the bomb's time came. The short fuse made a noise. They all heard it. The men down the hole did not even attempt to move; they knew instinctively they'd never make it. The man on the road made one wild fast step . . .

The cat heard it, too; the noise of the burning fuse sounded a bit like the noise another threatening cat makes. Her muscles were tensed for flight already, from the tension she could feel in the bomb disposal men. The man's sudden step scared her. She turned and made two long convulsive leaps . . .

The men's bodies were heavy, inert. The force of the explosion blew them to tiny fragments. Even the man on the road was blown into eight separate pieces; head, torso, limbs flew up like curving birds.

Lord Gort was twelve feet further away and already moving, and comparatively light and unresisting. The blast picked her up bodily in one piece, threw her sixty feet into the air. It blinded her, deafened her and singed her fur. But even in that wretched state, as she felt herself starting to fall earthwards again, her body began to twist on itself instinctively, so that she would land feet-first. Instinctively, too, she spread her legs wide like a flying squirrel, so that her soft folds of skin would act as a parachute.

It could still have gone ill with her. Had she fallen on the iron railings of the little park, she would have died a slow death, impaled on a spike. If she had fallen three yards further on she would have landed in the icy waters of a bomb-crater. Cold and wet, as well as suffering from shock, nothing would've saved her on that winter's night. But she crashed down among the soft springy leaves of an evergreen laurel, and bounced off on to a nest of dead ornamental fern. She got up slowly, and seemed to stare around. But she was blind. And she could hear nothing.

A human would have screamed and gone mad. Even in a state of shock, Lord Gort remained objective. She nosed herself here and there; there was a bloody patch on her back, but when she licked it, it came off on her tongue, leaving whole wet fur underneath. She ate the bloody piece; she would probably have eaten it if it had been part of herself; but it wasn't. It was food.

She found herself whole, and able to walk. Because she had been facing away from the bomb, her lungs

171

were not exploded. She breathed normally. Her sense of smell was returning, though it was choked with the smell of the explosion at first. Her fur smelt evil with chemicals. But she had her sense of smell to guide her, and that was far more important than sight or hearing. She had her sense of touch, too. Nothing could touch the tips of her fur but she knew it. Nothing could touch the tips of the whiskers about her mouth and above her eyes but she knew it. Like a half-crippled ship, she was still navigable.

She knew from the vibrations on the tips of her fur that it was starting to rain. She must find shelter; she must *not* get wet. And from her right came a smell of explosive, but also of dry dust, dry wood and dusty draperies.

Tentatively she sniffed the park wall, walked her front paws up it, and slipped through the iron railings that had nearly disembowelled her. She smelt the oil and petrol smell of the road, felt the sharpness of its gravel on her pads, and slipped across it quickly. She wormed through another set of railings and into the dry shelter of the bombed chapel. Some of the congregation had come and tried to salvage the curtains. But they were too badly torn, beyond hope, so they'd been tossed inside the skew-leaning pulpit and left. She had a half-roof over her; she had a warm dry nest as night and rain set in. She washed herself thoroughly all over, to comfort herself, and slept.

The wardens came, and the police. They found most of the parts of the soldier who had been on the road; they broke off when it got dark, and continued their search the following morning, when they found more. In the mortuary, a volunteer sorted out the bits and arranged them reverently in a coffin for burial. *Any* kind of body, in a sealed coffin, always comforted the relatives. For the other two soldiers, nothing could be done. In the hurry and confusion, some bits of them were buried with their friend.

For the next week of bitter January weather, the blind and deaf cat sallied forth from her pulpit and lived on bomb-death; then, her sight returning slowly, and her confidence with it, she roved further into the fields with their bomb-craters, and ate long-dead rook and wood-pigeon. She did not like it; but she survived.

After a fortnight, her sight was back to normal, and she was hunting living prey in the hedgerows again. She continued her journey. But she was still stone-deaf.

Mrs Wensley wakened around dawn, as she heard the first bomber returning. She kept her eyes shut, and settled her shoulders deeper under the blankets, and began to count.

Another single bomber. Then four together, landing quickly one after the other. Then a pause; then three more. The pattern was never the same two mornings running. Every time the pattern was different . . .

Twenty-five had flown off into the night. She had counted seventeen coming back when she heard the bomber in trouble, one engine cutting out and restarting. She lay with her fists clenched tight, willing it to land safely. It did. Though the screeching of its tyres on the runway was like a tormented soul, there was no crash.

173

She relaxed, and every muscle in her back and shoulders seemed to have its own new ache.

The twenty-first came in very low over the house, making the ewer rattle in the bowl on the washstand, filling the house with the roar of its engines. It should have terrified her, but it flooded her with peace.

That one was Geoff; Geoff letting her know he was home safe. He always did it. A bit like the victory-roll that fighter-pilots gave over their base after scoring a victory . . .

In Bomber Command, every time you came back safe was a victory.

At first, this roaring that filled the whole house had made little Jeff wake up and cry. But not now. He slept through it like a bomber pilot's son, as if he had learnt to welcome the sound of returning engines.

Mrs Wensley tried to stay awake to count the others in. She heard the twenty-third, as she slipped back guiltily into a deep, dreamless sleep, the best of the night. It seemed so wrong, not to stay awake to count the others in. They were all somebody's sons, somebody's husbands . . .

The next sound she heard was Geoffrey's old Bullnose Morris crunching on the gravel of the drive. Heard his soft flying-booted tread on the stairs. Heard little Jeff's door creak open.

She could picture the scene, because it was the same every time. Little Jeff asleep, turned to the right, one clenched hand in front of his snub nose. Geoffrey's great dirty finger poking the tiny fist, and the fist opening to enclose it. Then a long, long silence. Geoff just standing there, with his long, grubby white polo-neck sweater drooping miles below the belt of his battledress blouse.

Around them, the morning light would be strengthening on the shelves of toys. Toys made for little Jeff by the ground crew in idle times. Wooden railway engines, cars, shining Spitfires filed from aluminium. Geoffrey was popular with the ground crews, and sometimes he took Jeff with him to the base in the car. Florrie was always touched by the way the sweating, grimy men greeted the appearance of the small blond head. But they must all have children at home, and miss them . . .

Jeff liked the shining toys, but he didn't understand them at fourteen months. He pushed the trucks around, screaming wildly, and sometimes sucked the shining Spitfire. Only one toy had been denied him: a magnificent model of Geoffrey's own Wimpey, which had gone straight into the back of the dark cupboard.

'I don't want him flying when he grows up. I want him to be a biologist or something.'

Florrie worried that Geoffrey kept giving her instructions about what he wanted Jeff to be when he grew up; as if he didn't expect to be around himself . . .

She had also felt hurt, in the beginning, that Geoffrey always went to see little Jeff first, not her. But Geoffrey said Jeff helped him to 'rev down' as opposed to 'rev up'. When he had 'revved down' sufficiently, he would go downstairs and make a cup of tea, and bring it up to her . . .

She drifted off again, till she heard the rattle of teacups on the stairs. Geoff came in. The cups were

175

rattling on the tray a bit more than usual this morning. Must've been a rough night... but he looked the same as always, red-eyed, pale with weariness, half-dead.

'Morning, old lady.' He might have been greeting a dog he was fond of. He gave her outstretched cheek an absent-minded peck, and sat down heavily on the bed.

'You've done it, then,' she said. 'Twenty-five ops. A full tour of ops. When do we go on leave?' Already, her mind was on packing, on Dorset, on quiet walks by the river...

He sighed, in the way that always meant bad news.

'They want me to go back to the States. A buying mission. The Yanks are offering us two new crates: something called a Lockheed Ventura – a bigger version of the Hudson. And they've got a new version of the B–17 that they say can drop a bomb on a pickle-barrel from twenty thousand feet. They want my opinion as an operational user. They think I can talk the Yanks' lingo. I think they really want me because I can take the Yanks' hospitality and still be on my feet by the end...'

She said, 'Oh, *Geoff*...' She tried to crush down her disappointment. At least while he was in America he couldn't be killed over Germany. Not that anyone ever mentioned getting killed. In Geoff's new lingo, you 'bought it' or 'went for a Burton' or 'your number came up' or you 'pranged'. To hear Geoff talk, the air war was a gigantic farce, where the bombers couldn't find their targets in the dark, and the night-fighters couldn't find the bombers. Where the big events were crews who crash-landed in

Cabinet ministers' private grounds, and drank champagne for breakfast; or crash-landed on the main Lincoln road, and held up the traffic for an hour; or landed on a WRNS base, and were not seen again for twenty-four hours . . . All one great big male joke.

Except the crews who didn't come back at all; who disappeared in a sudden fireball over the marshalling yards at Hamm.

But nobody mentioned those.

He turned his back to get undressed. 'You go back to Dorset on your own, old lady. I'll try to join you there . . .'

'How long will you be gone?'

'At least a month. The Yanks do love *talking* . . .'

Then he came into bed, looking like a weary boy in his striped pyjamas. She put her arms around him. He took several enormous breaths, like a man about to dive into a deep pool, and was suddenly asleep.

This was the best time. This was the time she really had him back. She studied his sleeping face carefully in the dim, curtained light, tracing the slow growth of lines, the slight deepening of hollows. At least he'd eat well in America . . .

Then young Jeff woke up, and began yelling for his breakfast, and the best time was over for another day. When Geoff woke up at tea-time, he'd be starting to put on his wisecracking RAF face again, ready for the even younger men who thought he was God. In front of whom she too had to act normally, even when she felt like screaming.

It would be good to get away to the peace of Dorset.

18

Lord Gort was only a hundred yards from the house when Geoff's Bullnose Morris swept by her in the lane, forcing her up on to the long, dead grass of the verge. Geoff might have seen her, had his mind not already been on America.

Lord Gort was far too weary to start chasing the familiar car. Often, in the old days, her master had gone out in it, and soon returned. She went on to the house, and sniffed long under the locked front and back doors. The scent of her master was reassuringly fresh; and the smell of her mistress and the disliked baby. She waited patiently in the freezing garden, taking what shelter she could under a hedge. She watched an aircraft taking off, idly. And then she got the dreadful sense of her master going further and further away. Again. She hunched under the bleak twigs, head down, frown creasing her forehead, as near despair as she had ever been.

By nightfall, he had passed totally beyond her ken. She knew there was no point in waiting any more. From across the airfield came the faint, tempting smells from the aircrew messes and the greasy cookhouse. She headed in that direction in the end, having nothing better to do. But the walk seemed endless, and a north-east wind straight from the Steppes of Russia blew across the airfield and dispersals, with frost on its back. And she had eaten fairly recently; a dead rabbit by the roadside, killed by an RAF truck. Shelter was what she needed, as the wind blew ever colder.

By some unforgivable carelessness, the ground crew of B-Baker had left the access-hatch open and the access-ladder in place, after their final check-ups. Attracted like all cats by a dark, mysterious hole, Lord Gort climbed aboard. She sniffed carefully up and down the dark fuselage, and settled among the piled red blankets of the rest-bed near the tail, pounding and burrowing deeper and deeper between them. Thus, snug and warm, she slept.

When the aircrew climbed aboard for the op, she didn't stir. She had no mind to be thrown out into the freezing night. She couldn't hear a thing, being still totally deaf from the bomb; but she felt the swing and sway of the frail airframe under their weight. She just snuggled deeper, hoping they would go away and leave her in peace.

The engines were run up for the pre-flight checks; the noise filled the aircraft like a hurricane. The crew couldn't hear each other speak or even shout, six inches away, except through the earphones of the intercom. The noise should have driven Lord Gort from the plane; should have driven her mad, for a cat's hearing is far more acute than a man's. But she was completely deaf. The noise came to her only as a vibration through the blankets and her fur.

The bomber got the green Very light and took off and began to climb to its operational height. Lord Gort should have died then. For the operational height that night was twenty-two thousand feet. At

179

that height the crew could only breathe through their oxygen masks, and the lack of air would have made Lord Gort drown in the mass of bloody pink foam that would have filled her exploding lungs.

But the pilot and skipper, Gregson, flew according to the gospel of the famous Mickey Martin at only seven thousand feet. At that height, the light ack-ack was losing its power, and the heavy stuff would be aimed at the main bomber-stream at twenty-two thousand. Also, the night-fighters would be hunting around the edges of the main bomber-stream. So Lord Gort dozed safely on.

It was the cold that finally drove her out. Her nose, acutely sensitive to the least variation in temperature, told her it was warmer astern. Tommy Harrison, the rear-gunner had left his pair of armoured doors a touch open. She slipped through and on to his knee, as if he were sitting at his own fireside.

Tommy was in his usual state of sheer terror. Being a rear-gunner was the worst job in a very frightening trade. At least the crew in front had company. The wireless op sat with the navigator, and the skipper had the flight engineer leaning over his shoulder and the bomb-aimer sitting at his feet. Tommy sat alone at the end of the long, fragile tube of metal and canvas, down which an icy gale howled, feeling the loneliest man in the world. And if a night-fighter attacked, it would attack from the rear. The rear-gunner bought it first. Quite often planes came back almost untouched, with the rest of the crew very glad to be alive still, and the rear-gunner smeared all over the reddened Perspex of his turret, behind his armoured doors which had stopped the bullets reaching the rest of the crew.

But, if Tommy was scared, he was also superstitious. He truly believed that black cats were lucky. Being a Catholic, too, he thought that God had sent him the black cat as a blessed miracle. He suddenly knew that God would look after him that night and he would come home safe.

He had a lot to offer Lord Gort in return. He'd detached the nozzle of the hot-air hose and shoved it down his right flying-boot, so the hot air would flow up nicely round his crotch. Lord Gort, on his lap, got the full benefit. And of course Tommy, to calm his rumbling stomach, was starting to nibble nervously at his huge greasy pack of sandwiches ...

Lord Gort ate heartily; in return, her large furry body insulated him where it mattered most. The pair of them were in Heaven. Till Tommy hit his first problem.

They were halfway over the North Sea by that time; time to test his guns. He put it off as long as he could, scared the extra din and flashes would scare her away. But, in the end, those twin-Brownings were all that stood between him and a nasty end. So he kept one caressing hand on Lord Gort and fired.

She didn't flinch an inch, only watched the lines of red tracer curving away behind with an interested lift of her head. It was then he realized she was deaf. How else could she have put up with the endless blanketing roar of the engines without going mad?

The skipper made landfall over the island of Texel. For once the navigator had got it right. The bomber banked to starboard, and headed south over the

181

black quietness of the Zuyder Zee. Not much flak there, except for a few useless flakships whose tracer seemed to be heading straight for you, but always flicked astern at the last moment. Tommy noticed that Lord Gort was fascinated by the yellow and red balls; she didn't shiver, but she *quivered* with excitement, sometimes dabbing out a paw at the Perspex of the turret as the balls floated past.

Jerry put up quite a firework display, as they passed between Nijmegen and Arnhem; Lord Gort pouncing upwards at the big flashes made by the heavy flak, far overhead. Then they were into the last quiet stretch before the Ruhr, when they were flying alone through an empty moonlit cloudscape, and the war might have been on another planet.

That was the dangerous bit; that was when rear-gunners fell asleep, in the relief that followed tension. That was when the night-fighters came. The skipper's voice crackled down the intercom, asking Tommy if he was OK. The skipper was good; he talked to you often, about nothing really, just to stop you feeling lonely. Nagged you like a wife, just to make sure you stayed awake. Tommy felt tempted to tell him about the cat, but he was scared that Skip might send somebody to take the cat away from him. He didn't feel inclined to share his luck at this stage.

Lord Gort got a bit bored; she'd enjoyed the flashing lights; she looked for more.

And suddenly she seemed to see something that Tommy couldn't. She tensed, flicked her head from side to side as if to get a better view, then dabbed out swift as lightning with her right paw, against the Perspex of the turret window.

Tommy looked to see where she'd dabbed; he couldn't see a bloody thing.

She tensed and dabbed out again. Still he couldn't see anything. He wondered if it was one of those tiny black gnats you got in Lincolnshire in summer; the ones cats chase when you think they're chasing nothing. Hibernating in the plane for the winter and revived by the heat of the air-hose.

And then Lord Gort dabbed a third time, and he saw it. Even smaller than a gnat on the Perspex. A pale grey shape against the clouds below that could only be a Jerry night-fighter. Well out of range, but hoping to creep up into the blind spot beneath the Wimpey. Without Lord Gort he would never have seen it. But now he had seen it, he had the edge. God had sent him Lord Gort for luck that night. For once, he felt invincible.

He didn't warn his skipper, like he should have done, so the skipper could have taken evasive action. No, God was going to put this murderous gnat right on to the end of his gun barrels. He eased the turret round, very slowly and gingerly, so Jerry wouldn't guess he'd been rumbled. Got Jerry in his ring-sight and watched him grow.

This Jerry was one of the best, a real craftsman. Probably one of their aces, with dozens of poor sodding Whitleys and Wimpeys to his credit. He took advantage of every wisp of cloud to get nearer without being spotted. Soon Tommy could see he was an Me 110, covered in pale grey spotted camouflage that was nearly invisible against moonlit clouds. More radio antennae bristling from its nose than a rat has whiskers. No front guns to worry about, then! Only the upward-firing cannons fixed behind the cockpit, which Jerry couldn't use until he was directly underneath them. Schragemusik, the intelligence officer said the Jerries called them. Organ-music. We'll see who gets organ-music this time, you bastard.

Tommy felt *combined* with the cat. The cat had ceased to dab at the Perspex, as Jerry came nearer, but she was peering to the right round the gun-mountings to keep Jerry in view. She was pounding on his knees with claws that expanded and contracted; Tommy could feel the claws on his skin, through the thickness of his trousers. He could feel the cat's backside wriggling against his chest, against the parachute straps and Mae West.

But the cat was patient; and her hunting patience, her icy joy passed through to Tommy. Coldly he let the Jerry get nearer, till he could see the pilot's face, looking upward; till he could read the plane's registration numbers.

Then the Jerry seemed to sense danger; there was a flick of movement in the control-surfaces at the tips of his wings . . .

Tommy put a five-second burst straight into the Jerry's cockpit. He saw the cockpit-cover fly apart like a shower of silver ice. But the fighter went steadily boring on, getting beneath him. Like swatting a half-dead fly a second time, Tommy gave him another five-second burst into the port engine, and the fire grew and grew.

The skipper nearly had a heart attack. What with Tommy screaming, 'I've got him, Skip, I've got him,' and this burning Jerry crate flying out directly under his nose. The skipper threw the Wimpey upwards and to port, before the fighter blew up and took them all with him. Tommy heard the Elsan break loose, and smelt the pong filling the aircraft. Then the Jerry blew up like an exploding star, blinding everybody on the bomber for two or three minutes.

After that the bomb-run over Düsseldorf was almost an anti-climax.

Going home, it was like a party. Fourteen aircraft the squadron had lost, and this was the first night-fighter it had ever done for. The skipper had a terrible job, getting everyone to keep on looking out of the Perspex going home. If they'd had drink aboard, they'd have got drunk.

It wasn't until after they'd left the Dutch coast that Tommy told them about the black cat sitting on his knee.

'Poor sod,' said the skipper. 'It's been too much for him. He'll be reporting magic carpets next.'

19

They were the last home. They burst into the debriefing hall like a happy gale. All the other crews were still there, drinking their breakfast, which was supposed to be coffee, but was always liberally reinforced with something stronger. And waiting to find out who had bought it.

They had the little WAAF debriefing officer nearly in tears.

'We gotta night-fighter,' announced Tommy. 'This cat got it!' He pointed to Lord Gort who was hanging around his neck. Lord Gort blinked at the lady amiably. But the WAAF thought they were having her on, and summoned her boss, who summoned Groupie. Everyone gathered round, open-mouthed.

The group captain had never heard anything so ridiculous in his life; it was a long time before he believed it. And when he did believe it, he grew even more worried. What price airfield security, if stray cats could stow away on Wimpeys? How good was a rear-gunner who was obsessed with playing with a cat? What in hell would Bomber Command say, if it ever reached their ears?

But he also weighed up the sea of grinning faces. There hadn't been much to grin about at South Wedderby that winter. The huts were stinkers; the air-crew froze on the ground and in the air, day and night. The local pubs were hovels and the most attractive local females were the horses. And the bombing of Germany was a flop. Half the crews never even found their targets. Of those who did, only half dropped their bombs within five miles of it. But still the losses mounted. More aircrew were getting killed than Jerry civilians . . .

'Put the bloody animal on the crew-roster. Shilling a day for aircrew rations. Those Wimpeys are full of bloody mice . . .'

That got a laugh. Everybody knew no mouse that valued its life would go near a Wimpey, sandwich crumbs or no sandwich crumbs.

Lord Gort began to work her old magic; it just so happened that the night she got the fighter every single bomber had returned undamaged, for the first time in weeks. Everybody *knew* that black cats were lucky!

She slept with Tommy; she ate with Tommy. But in the mess hall, during an ops breakfast, she'd jump from table to table and get spoiled rotten with bacon rind and even whole lumps of bacon. Nobody had much appetite at an ops breakfast. She grew enormously plump; her fur went almost greasy with good living.

Everybody had to stroke her before they flew. If she dropped a whisker, it was snatched up and put in a battledress pocket carefully. Especially after she helped Tommy get his second Jerry fighter.

All aircrew were mascot mad. The new wingco wouldn't fly without his old golf umbrella; said he could use it if his chute failed to open. But the night his ground crew mislaid it he went as white as a sheet and threw up then and there on the tarmac. And wrote off a brand-new Wimpey with the lousiest return landing anybody had ever seen. Everybody had mascots: rabbit's feet, golliwogs, a pair of silk knickers.

But, desperate as everyone was for a bit of Lord Gort, she was treated with respect. If they stroked her and one or two of her hairs came off on their hands, that was their good luck. But only a fool would try to pull hairs out of her. Good luck couldn't be *stolen*.

As the crew of G-George found when they tried to kidnap her.

Lord Gort had been missing all day; the crew had had to *carry* Tommy out to the plane, because he was quite certain that, without her, he was in for the chop. Then, as they were waiting their turn for take-off they saw G-George trying to sneak past and jump the queue. That was G-George's undoing. Tommy saw it quite clearly because it was bright moonlight. Wimpeys had those little triangular windows all along their sides. Lord Gort's face appeared at one of them. And those windows were just stitched-on celluloid. They saw her paws scrabbling, then the window was out, and Lord Gort was leaping towards them like a Derby winner, through the moving under-carriage wheels and vicious whirling props. Tommy swung his turret hard left, exposing the armoured doors behind him. He opened the doors and she jumped in, and they went off to Essen.

Lord Gort got her third Jerry that night. Word of her fame got beyond the station, through aircrew talking in pubs. Reporters turned up and slipped the crew a fiver to smuggle them on to the airfield with a photographer. Articles appeared in the local then the national press, with a photo of Lord Gort clinging on to Tommy for grim death, under the daft headline:

LORD GORT HUNTS THE HUN!

The censors let it through; it was good for civilian morale. The crew held their breath, awaiting the chop from Bomber Command. A phone call did come through from Bomber Command, asking if the story were true. Then silence. Bomber Command was reported as thinking it was quite amusing. They, too, understood the need to keep up crew morale. Lord Gort flew on.

Until the night she walked aboard and walked off again. Gregson was just revving up the engines when she walked to the exit-hatch and began to claw at it, and gave little silent miaows through the roar of the engines, *pleading* to be out.

The crew argued so much over the intercom that it got noticed in the control tower. Oddly enough, it was Tommy who settled it.

'She volunteered to fly, and she can bloody volunteer out. I'm not taking her against her will.' Nobody stopped him as he undid the door-clips and she dropped to the ground and shot off to the warmth of the ground crew's hut.

They took off and climbed to seven thousand feet in a silence like a funeral.

Then the flight-engineer, glancing at the dials, said, 'Port engine's acting up, Skip!'

It was, a fraction. Engine temperature a little too

189

hot; losing a few revs then gaining a few too many, without anyone touching the throttle. It was the kind of acting-up that usually stopped, if you flew on for a bit. They'd been to Berlin and back with worse. And certainly it was the kind of fault that would vanish the moment they turned back for the airfield. Leaving them with egg all over their faces, and a very nasty interview with Groupie in the morning. That was always the way it went when a crew's nerve started to go: bit of untraceable engine trouble; bit of undefined radio trouble . . . the slippery slope which ended with aircrew lying in their bunks, gibbering like babies under the bedclothes till they came to take them away and court-martial them for lack of moral fibre or LMF, and reduce them all to the rank of AC2 and put them on permanent duty cleaning air-field bogs . . .

They flew out over the North Sea; it looked very empty and cold in the moonlight.

Then Tommy said over the intercom, 'She was always keen to come before, Skipper. She *knows* something . . .'

'Or she wanted a pee,' snarled Gregson. '*Or* she's on heat and going courting . . .'

'She pees on board – haven't you smelt it? And she was keen enough to come afore you revved the engines . . .'

Then the bomb-aimer said, 'We've done twenty-three missions. They owe us one . . .'

With a curse, Gregson swung the plane violently to port in a half-circle, like a fighter was after him.

The moment they turned back, the engine settled

down and ran as sweet as a sewing machine, all the way home.

They were all in Groupie's office the following morning, having a very nasty strip torn off, when they heard the bang, right through the brick walls. They all ran out together, Groupie leading; but across the airfield, in her dispersal, B-Baker was already a write-off. It turned out afterwards that the ground-crew sergeant had been revving that port engine, to prove there was nothing wrong with his darling. When a prop-blade snapped clean off at the shaft. Cut straight through the cockpit, shaving off a slice of his backside, and straight out the other side into the main petrol tank of the starboard wing. Which promptly took fire. The sergeant got away with a well-singed skin and one and a half buttocks. He was lucky; he was on the ground at the time. In the air, the crew wouldn't have had a prayer . . .

There was a lot of argument about how Lord Gort had known. Some clever-cuts reckoned that she'd felt the vibrations from the duff propeller, through the air-frame and the pads of her feet, the moment Gregson began to rev up. But most people reckoned she just *knew*.

From being a mascot, from being a heroine, Lord Gort became a god with knowledge of life and death. When people stroked her, they stroked with awe now; they stroked with fear.

Then came the matter of O-Oboe.

She had always spent a lot of her day on the aircraft at their dispersals. The six-foot jump to the wing-root was nothing to her, even in her newly plump state. She would flirt with the ground crews as they worked on the engines, and never say no to grub. Then she would trot along the top of the fuselage and sit washing herself, in a brief glimpse of March sun, on top of a cockpit canopy. On any of the planes, not just the new B-Baker. The other crews liked it; they reckoned she was spreading her luck around.

And it was a fact, as everybody said, that since she had come the squadron hadn't lost a single crate. Of course, it was one of those spells of luck that any squadron has. That and the aircraft not flying many missions, because of bad weather. But frightened men grasp at straws. Frightened men *make* gods . . .

And Lord Gort grew more fond of O-Oboe than any other plane except B-Baker. For one thing, it stood next to B-Baker on dispersal. For another, one of O-Oboe's ground crew had a lady-friend in the village who slipped him packets of salty fat pork sandwiches.

Until the fatal day when the ground-crew sergeant of O-Oboe came to Gregson, as he sat sweating over a crew-return in the flight office.

'Think your cat's ill, sir. We can't do nothing with her.'

All the crew hurried over to O-Oboe. Lord Gort sat on the cockpit canopy, hunched up, eyes closed, brow furrowed. Tommy climbed up and got her down in the end, because for once she wouldn't come when they beckoned, or even open her eyes. They took her back to the flight office, and examined her anxiously. Her legs worked all right. (How else could she have climbed up there?) Nobody could feel anything broken; she didn't cry or flinch when they handled her. She purred, in a half-hearted sort of way, but her nose was dry and slightly warm.

'Eaten something she shouldn't,' said Gregson. That was the last sensible thing anybody said. They gave her a saucer of milk; she drank a bit, and that satisfied them she wasn't ill. They forgot about it.

Ten minutes later, she was back on top of O-Oboe in the same hunched, furrowed position.

Now Gregson had been right. Lord Gort *had* eaten something she shouldn't. In spite of an endless supply of wholesome sandwiches and bacon, for some feline reason of her own she had trifled with a crow killed by a whirling airscrew that had been lying dead on the tarmac for four days. She felt . . . off-colour. She had not felt like being stroked, fussed over and generally mucked about by everyone who met her. Which was why she had taken refuge on the cockpit canopy of O-Oboe.

And having been rudely and forcibly removed from there, with cat-like stubbornness she went straight back. She had no idea, of course, that in the minds of the airmen she was a goddess with knowledge of life and death. O-Oboe's ground crew cast her increasingly worried glances as they worked on the plane. Especially at her closed eyes and furrowed brow, the sign of pain in a cat.

'She's grievin',' said the airframe fitter.

'What the hell you mean, "grievin' "?' snapped the sergeant.

'She knows.'

'What the hell you mean, she *knows*?'

'She knows this crate's for the chop . . .'

'Don't talk so bloody wet . . .'

'She knew when B-Baker was going for a Burton . . .'

The sergeant, uneasy himself, couldn't think of any answer to that. He went and asked Gregson to come and take her away again.

'And for Christ's sake keep her locked up till the op starts, sir. She's making everybody nervous.'

They took her back to the flight office and tied her to the table with a bit of thin rope round her neck. They guarded the door as if the Waffen-SS were about to break in. Then the wingco came in in a fury with a complaint about low flying that had really nothing to do with them. And by the time they'd cooled him down, Lord Gort had slipped her collar and was gone out through the open transom window.

Back to her old place on O-Oboe. They got her down a third time, but by then the damage was done. Everyone on the airfield knew that Lord Gort knew that O-Oboe was for the chop that night.

It was the topic about which air-crew were at their most twitchy; where the most crazy rubbish was talked. There were bunks in the Nissen huts where every guy who dared sleep in them got the chop straight away. After a while, nobody would sleep in that bunk. There were whole Nissen huts where any crew that slept in them got the chop straight away. After a bit, a wise Groupie would turn that hut over to storing NAAFI supplies. There was even a most beautiful WAAF on the station, all of whose boy-friends got the chop. Nobody would go near her; in the end, lonely and in despair, she'd got herself pregnant by a local farmer, who married her and so solved the problem.

Nobody looked at O-Oboe's crew at the briefing. A sort of space opened up around them at ops breakfast, which was eaten at night, just before take-off. Everyone could tell, just by looking at them that they knew they'd had it.

They crashed on take-off. There was just one sheet of flame at the far end of the runway, where their full bomb-load went up. The state they were in, it really wasn't surprising.

After that, the ground crews took against Lord Gort. When she appeared round their aircraft while they were servicing it, they shooed her away. She didn't understand, and kept coming back. They began throwing nuts and bolts at her. From being the luck of the squadron, she became the angel of death. Gregson and his crew were puzzled when she limped into the flight office one day, covered with engine oil. But when she came in stinking of petrol, they knew the score. She had only been one well-struck match away from a hideous death.

The wingco told Gregson she'd have to go. Losses were climbing again, because the weather was better, and the wing was flying more ops. But the men blamed Lord Gort . . .

Tommy took her to live with an aunty of his in Doncaster. Gregson drove them across in his jeep. They sneaked out of Aunty's, leaving her asleep by a roaring fire, with a saucer of mince and a saucer of milk by her nose. They were sad, but they reckoned she'd done her bit for the War Effort.

Half an hour after they left, she vanished through Aunty's open bathroom window across the rooftops. Four nights later, she turned up at dispersals spot on time for the op. Forty miles was nothing to Lord Gort. They took her with them; they reckoned she'd be safer with the ack-ack and Jerry fighters . . .

It was to be her last op. A fresh target: the new U-boat pens at L'Orient, on the French coast. It should have been an easy one, sea all the way, after making their turn over a Coastal Command station near Land's End to fool the German radar. Out over the Bay of Biscay, then in over L'Orient at low altitude to keep on fooling the German radar.

But the German radar wasn't fooled. The gunners were waiting with their ack-ack guns at low angles. The flak was hell. Thirty seconds into the bomb-run, B-Baker took a 35mm cannon-shell amidships. The radio sets burst into flames. The bomb-aimer dropped his bombs outside the harbour, into the sea, just to get rid of them. They went skidding on over France with the flames chewing into the aluminium airframe, and Gregson yelling 'bail out, bail out' and fighting to get enough height on the plane, so that the parachutes would have a chance of opening.

Of all the things aircrew are terrified of, the worst is fire. They don't worry so much about being blown to bits because that's a quick death. But to die slowly, like a flaming torch, with your chute on fire, too, so you can't bail out . . . it can take a burning crate four minutes to hit the ground and merciful oblivion. So it was all the more credit to Gregson's navigator and wireless op that they fought the fire with anything they could find, even their gauntleted hands.

Fortunately, the fire burnt through the mountings of the radio sets and the radio sets went out of a gap in the fuselage, leaving a gaping hole and a hurricane of wind.

They were back over the Channel before Gregson sent the flight-engineer to check on the silence in Tommy's rear turret.

The turret was swung hard to the right, exposing the armoured doors. The armoured doors were open, and Tommy and Lord Gort were gone. Tommy had bailed out, and taken Lord Gort with him.

20

Tommy fell backwards through the open armoured doors and spun head over heels in a howling maelstrom of darkness and moonlight. A hurricane of wind tore at him, trying to rip Lord Gort from his arms. He knew he must pull the ring of his parachute instantly, or he'd hit the ground before it opened and they'd both splatter. But if he freed one hand to find it, he might lose Lord Gort, and Lord Gort was his luck . . .

Lord Gort had only one instinct in the maelstrom; to stick her claws as hard as she could into Tommy and hang on to the last solid thing in the world.

Desperately, Tommy released his grip on Lord Gort with his right hand and groped for the ring. He couldn't find it; it wasn't where it ought to be. Lord Gort panicked, and tried to scramble up on to his shoulder. Tommy grabbed with his right hand again, and found the ring miraculously, under Lord Gort's fur. He pulled it, and redoubled his grip on the cat, in a kind of stranglehold that made Lord Gort squirm like an eel in terror.

The upward pull as the chute opened was incredible. Lord Gort shot down through his arms. Only a desperate grab held on to one hind leg. Lord Gort kicked and swung, then bent her body double and clawed her way up Tommy's legs, his chest, his face, gouging so deep Tommy almost lost an eye.

And then they were at rest, in harmony, swaying down softly into a peaceful landscape of fields without hedges and a road lined with poplars all the way to the horizon. Lord Gort gave a short puzzled purr; she was trembling all over.

Then the ground suddenly accelerated towards them. Tommy bent his legs as he'd been taught, hit and rolled. He lost his hold on Lord Gort in the confusion. Tommy, staring about in bewilderment, thought he saw her about ten yards away, across the ploughed field. Then he heard voices coming towards him; soft excited voices.

Lord Gort took one startled look in that direction, and vanished silently into a ditch. Where she shook her head, as if in bewilderment, till her ears rattled. There was a feeling of something loose inside her right ear, and very, very faintly sounds were beginning to filter in. The rush of air in the parachute drop, the jerk of gravity as the chute opened, or her own convulsive kicking had loosened something in her right ear tube that the blast of the bomb had blocked. She could hear again, though very poorly; much less well than a human being.

Tommy went on lying in the soft furrows. He knew he should get up, hide his chute, make for cover, run like hell. But Lord Gort was gone; his luck was gone. The voices were almost upon him; everything was happening too fast for him to keep up. So he just sat, weeping uncontrollably.

Florrie spent a month with her mother, then headed

up north to South Wedderby again, reflecting that the grass wasn't always greener on the other side of the fence. Her mother had been busy non-stop: evacuee's welfare, WVS, savings clubs; she had turned herself into a relentless machine against Hitler. The house at Beaminster was in a terrible state, the carpet worn into holes on the stairs, rude and cheeky children everywhere, who were not above giving Jeff a spiteful pinch as he slept in his pram. The kitchen was as full as ever of evacuee mums who by now thought they owned the place and looked on Florrie as the outsider. At least at South Wedderby she had the peace of her own home, and the respect owed to a wing-commander's wife. She would wait for Geoffrey there.

Actually, it wasn't so bad at South Wedderby now. There were daffodils in the garden, and a faint smell of spring green coming from the Fenland fields. She spent a lot of time in the garden when it was fine, rescuing what plants were left from the stranglehold of weeds, giving the old rose trees a belated pruning with a stout pair of kitchen scissors, while Jeff slept or gurgled in his pram, under the flowering cherry, or got himself filthy helping her. With Geoffrey away, the airfield wasn't a frightening place. It was distant, remote, rather meaningless. The bombers still flew out late and came home early, but because Geoff was not aboard, she gave up counting them. Simply turned her back on the distant airfield buildings.

Until one morning she looked up from weeding the crazy-paving path to see Groupie coming through the gate, looking rather solemn . . .

Her heart lurched, but he called swiftly, 'It's all right; he's not badly hurt.'

She made him a cup of tea with unsteady hands. Groupie stood by her, massive, grey as a badger, fiddling with his cap and looking so gentle that none of the aircrew would have believed it.

'It's his hand,' he said. 'He's lost two fingers; the index and the next one. Right hand. I'm afraid his flying days are over . . . well . . . perhaps in time he'll be able to manage a Tiger Moth or something small like that . . . I know how he loves flying . . . We shan't be able to keep him out of the air for long. But as for flying the big stuff . . . he's had it. Stupid accident really. Going round an American aircraft factory. They let him try using a mechanical press . . . the safety-guard was defective or something. Took off his two fingers as clean as a whistle. Seems odd . . . he came through all those missions and then it has to happen among friends.'

She asked him if he took sugar. Then said, 'What'll happen to him now?'

'Fly a desk for the rest of the war, I suppose. Job like mine. Sending off the young fellers to do your fighting for you. Writing to their parents when they don't come back. We'll be opening up a lot of new airfields – the RAF's expanding like billy-o. He won't like it, but he'll do it well. The young aircrew will respect him, because he'll know what he's talking about – he's been through it. But it's a damn depressing job . . .' Groupie stirred his tea to work off his feelings, for the third time. In spite of his girth, he had once flown Bristol fighters in World War I.

Mrs Wensley felt split in half. In her mind's eye she could see Geoffrey's right hand, lean, brown, sinewy. A pair of scissors like those she'd just used for pruning the roses suddenly cut off first one finger, then another. No blood seemed to flow.

But, within her, her heart soared. Geoff was going to *live*. No more nights waiting for . . .

'Don't know what he'll do after the war,' said Groupie fretfully. 'Can't see him staying in the R A F. He's not cut out for a desk-wallah!'

She heard him out patiently; saw him off through the gate, and waved back as he turned three times to wave. The sun came out; the daffodils bent double in the cold wind.

We're going to have a spring, she thought. *We're* going to have a spring.

Lord Gort watched silently, intently, as the men came and took Tommy away. Their voices *sounded* friendly, but they made the wrong kind of sounds: musical liquid sounds that rose and fell dramatically, even when they tried to keep them low and quiet. These new men were also excited, scared. The smell of their fear came to Lord Gort where she lay. *All* their smells were strange.

Lord Gort had had enough strangeness and fear for one night, so she lay low; even the grass in the ditch smelt strange. She was suddenly *very* tired. Idly she watched one of the men gather up and fold the white billowing mass that had been Tommy's parachute. Then she followed Tommy's trail of scent to a house. She listened, and heard his voice among other voices. Then she found a nook high up in a barn and slept.

A fortnight later, Tommy was still in France. Sitting on a piece of filthy rug in a damp hole dug in the ground under a hen-cree, somewhere south-east of Bordeaux. Above his head, the white French chickens clucked sleepily. The smell of their droppings was awful.

He couldn't sleep for the cold, and the aches in his body. He could tell from a grey light coming through the cracks in the floor of the hen-cree that it was nearly dawn. He wondered how often he would be terrified today. At first, it had been the Germans; passing the Germans. Nazis, just like in the newsreels, except these Germans were in full colour, not black and white. Germans who scratched their arses as they stood on street corners watching you. Belched and shouted jokes to each other and laughed and looked very much at home. Far more real and scary than the flak over the Ruhr.

He'd been terrified of falling off his bike as he passed them, that horrible old French bike with twenty-eight-inch wheels and sit-up-and-beg handlebars and a rusty chain that kept on threatening to jump off the chainwheel. He'd been told never to look at the Germans; no Frenchman did. Catch their eye, and they might stop you and ask for your *carte d'identité* out of sheer bloody-mindedness and boredom.

He kept on trying to ride on the wrong side of the road. Keep right, he muttered to himself. Keep *right*. Traffic kept on coming at him from the wrong side.

One terrifying day he'd had a puncture, and the guide in front had ridden on without him and not come back for an hour . . .

Now, in Unoccupied France, the Germans were gone. But they said the Vichy police were worse. They had sharper eyes; unlike the Germans, they knew what a typical Frenchman looked like . . . they were bastards.

He'd insisted on keeping his RAF uniform. If they caught aircrew without it, they shot them as spies. His helpers had dyed the bottom of the trousers black; given him a ragged old overcoat and cracked cheap French shoes and a beret that was too big and always threatening to blow off as he rode. He knew he made it harder for them, more dangerous, by insisting on the uniform. But he was *not* going to be shot as a spy.

It was very lonely. His helpers constantly argued over him in French, so he couldn't understand a word, only try to interpret the looks they gave him, and the sound of their voices. He didn't feel they liked him very much; he thought some of them argued in favour of abandoning him to his own devices.

He wondered miserably what had happened to Lord Gort. He'd hardly seen a cat in his whole journey. They said the French in the cities were eating cats because they were starving. When they served rabbit pie in restaurants, the customers made little miaow-noises with their mouths . . .

He wondered how many more days. That was the only bright spot.

Late yesterday afternoon, in the clear sunset, he had seen, very distantly – almost like clouds – snow-capped mountains. The Pyrenees. Beyond lay Spain. Where, unlike the French, they wouldn't hand you back to the Germans. Just lock you up in a lousy Spanish flea-ridden prison till the end of the war.

But, beyond Spain, Portugal, where they actually liked the British, on the quiet. Once you were in Portugal, you were home and dry. Unless the Jerry fighters caught the plane flying you home across the Bay . . .

He wasn't even *halfway* home yet. Fourteen days of near shitting yourself ten times a day, and not even halfway home. He wished he was more of a hero.

There came a scrabbling at the side of the hut, making him jump. Above, the hens began to make a nervous clucking. A tiny chink of light appeared. Two black paws, scrabbling soil. A black soily nose, sniffing . . .

Christ, it was Lord Gort. All this way, she had followed him.

His heart leapt with new hope. His luck had not given out. But he pushed at her nose fiercely through the small hole she had made.

'Bugger off, you silly cow. If they catch you, they'll *eat* you!'

It almost seemed she understood. The black nose vanished and did not return. He began to wonder if it *had* been Lord Gort at all. There were plenty of black cats in the world. Maybe this was a local, after a nice French chicken . . .

Lord Gort, satisfied that she had found her person, retired to a discreet distance down a long-empty rabbit hole, and slept, content.

*

A week later, Tommy was crouching terrified in a ditch. Beyond the ditch, the Pyrenees loomed gigantic and black against the night sky. He was only eight miles from Spain; eight miles from freedom.

But there was a Vichy patrol working across the hillside towards them; a Vichy patrol where there should not have been a Vichy patrol. And the ditch where he crouched with his French Basque guide was so shallow, only a fool could fail to see him. And the last thing the Vichy frontier patrols were were fools. Tommy pressed his face into the dry dead weeds at the bottom of the ditch, smelling the smell of French earth that after three weeks was still alien to him. And he prayed. Not now! Not after all that cycling, all that terror, all that passing of Germans. Not back to Nazi Germany and the Gestapo and God knew what . . .

The patrol swished towards them through the long grass. He could hear four pairs of boots, thudding on the turf. He heard their voices, raised in incomprehensible foreign argument. Maybe the argument would carry them past. At least they would pass twenty yards away . . .

Three pairs of boots passed; or was it four? It was so hard to tell. The sound of them faded. He had an unbearable desire to look up; but the hand of his guide, hard on his neck, pressed his face deeper into the ditch.

There was still one guard there, standing motionless, whistling softly under his breath. Watching, listening. A man sharper than the others; a man with an unfair advantage, who sensed with an unknown sense that there was a living thing in the silent unstirring ditch . . . Tommy prepared to get up, raise his hands, be manhandled, humiliated. That was becoming easier to face than going on lying silent in the ditch.

Then a rustle to his left. Something getting out of the ditch. Something unaccountable that shouldn't be there.

'Ah!' said the frontier guard, delighted. 'Minou, Minou, Minou!'

A burst of laughter and chatter. What was it that had come out of the ditch to Tommy's left? A girl? The guard's girlfriend? He sounded ecstatic enough . . .

Then, shouting from the rest of the patrol, summoning the last guard on impatiently.

'Au 'voir, Minou.' And his footsteps, too, were thudding away.

Tommy let out a deep, shuddering breath. 'What was it?'

The guide laughed shakily; his life had been on the chopping block, too.

'A black cat, m'sieur. We have been saved by a black cat with a rat in her mouth. The guard knew there was something living here. The cat satisfied him. He has gone away happy, justified. He is obviously a lover of cats. The others called to him that he should either shoot the cat for eating, or take it to bed with him . . . We are safe now; that will be the only patrol tonight. Allons . . .'

Lord Gort was slow to follow; Tommy's scent left a clear trail in the warm, damp night air. And she had caught a rat that she intended to enjoy at leisure. She had also enjoyed meeting the frontier guard. He

207

had approved of her, smelt good. She had gone to him because he whistled to her, like her old master had done, so long ago.

Lord Gort finished the rat and trotted on, climbing steadily all the way. She caught up with Tommy and the guide, before they reached the high frontier. She was only thirty yards behind, when they all crossed the invisible line, on the other side of which was a land where they did not hand young fliers back to the Gestapo, and were not so hungry that they needed to eat cats; usually.

The man from the British consulate in Lisbon who dealt with returning fliers shifted in his highly polished shoes uneasily, and stared at the haggard young air-gunner in front of him. The boy was in a terrible state; by this time, after a week in Portugal, they were usually starting to get their nerve back. But not this one. He was sweating, though it was still early morning, and not hot; he twisted his dirty old beret with thin hands that were never still.

'A cat?' asked the man from the consulate, incredulously. 'A cat that flew with you in a Wellington bomber? That shot down German night-fighters? That saved you from capture on the French frontier?'

'Yeh,' said Tommy, staring at the floor. He knew he hadn't told his story very well; his mind kept going fuzzy. 'And she's kept on following me since then. I keep on seeing her in the distance . . .'

'But, my dear young man, Portugal is full of cats, including black ones. I saw one myself, on my way here this morning . . .'

'Did it have a brown collar?' asked Tommy, anxiously leaning forward. 'And a little brass name-tag?'

'I didn't notice. I had other things on my mind,' said the man from the consulate, though he had an uneasy feeling that the black cat he had seen *did* have something round its neck. Anyway, he had not come to have this ridiculous discussion about black cats. His job was to get this young airman home before he cracked up *completely*, and had to be hospitalised to the embarrassment of both governments.

'Where did you see this black cat?' persisted Tommy. 'We've got to get her a flight home. I *can't* leave her here after all she's done for me . . .'

'Out of the question,' said the man from the consulate. 'There's no room for cats on that plane; there's hardly enough room for *people*. And of course it's *unthinkable*. There are regulations about rabies – the cat is probably rabid by this time. If it reached England, it would have to be *destroyed*.'

Tommy began to weep silently; he didn't make a noise, the tears just ran down his face. It seemed to keep on happening all the time, since he had reached Portugal.

The man from the consulate got up to go, scarlet with embarrassment. Englishmen did not cry; especially in front of Portuguese *women*.

After he had gone, the woman who ran the house clutched the sobbing Tommy to her capacious bosom. War was terrible; she hoped Portugal would never join in.

21

The fifth day Geoff was home, Groupie came to see him. Even though Geoff had ten days' sick leave still to run.

Geoff jumped out of the deckchair on the tiny lawn with a guilty start. He felt guilty about so many things. About his hand. How had he been so bloody careless as to get it in the sudden slicing agony of that American metal-press? If he'd *cared* it wouldn't have happened . . . Had he *wanted* it to happen? To get out of flying?

But he felt much more guilty about the airfield. Because he hated the airfield now. Out for a walk, he would go out of his way to avoid even the sight of the place.

Now he had no more need of courage, he found he had no courage left. He could see quite clearly how terrified he'd been from start to finish. The dashing young wing-commander had all been an act, a crazy, desperate act, and he could no longer see how he had ever kept it up for so long

And yet he was a Regular; the RAF had been his whole life . . .

He could hardly lift his eyes to look Groupie in the face.

'Sit you down, Geoff,' said Groupie gently. 'You look *bloody* tired.' He sat down himself, on the lush

May grass of the lawn, and pulled a few green blades up and inspected them, as if they were defective components. When he spoke, he was still looking at the blades of grass.

Please, thought Geoff. Please don't tell me what a loss I am to the RAF. Please don't tell me what a brilliant flying career has been ruined . . .

But Groupie's first words took him by surprise; they were completely off at a tangent.

'D'you know what that silly bastard Tomlinson's done? He goes on leave, and the first thing he does is to break both legs. Playing football with his son. Fell over the edge of a terrace on to a cucumber-frame. Won't be back for bloody months. Not that he was much good when he *was* here.'

Tomlinson was the Intelligence Officer to the wing. A fat, bumbling man, who was a standing joke with the pilots. He dropped his notes at every second ops briefing. If he said there was heavy flak to be expected, to the south of Osnabrück, there would be no flak. Where Tomlinson said there'd be no flak, there'd be hell to pay. 'According to Tomlinson' always got a laugh; but it was bitter laughter.

Groupie went on staring at the four blades of grass in his hand.

'I need a new Intelligence-wallah *now*, Geoff. Young Bailey's just not up to it; eighteen months under Tomlinson seems to have addled his brains. I'd like you to take on the job *now*, Geoff. Even before your leave's up. There's an op tonight . . .'

There was a long pause. Then Groupie said, 'I know it's not the same as flying. But you could save lives. You're ex-aircrew. You know the score. You know what awkward questions to ask at Group. And the aircrews will *listen* to you, because you *are* ex-aircrew. Will you do it? At least until Tomlinson gets back? Job's hardly strenuous . . .'

Geoff looked at Groupie. Groupie's eyes were blue and unfathomable. Had Groupie guessed he was cowering here at home, hating the RAF, hating the airfield, the dark, vomit-smelling bombers squatting at their dispersals?

'If you don't do this,' said Groupie, 'they intend to make a hero out of you. Give you the Distin-guished Flying Cross and send you on a tour of the aircraft-factories, telling them what a grand job they're doing, and how we're winning the war in the air over Europe . . .'

'Christ . . .' Geoff spat the word out, as if he were being sick.

'You'll do it, then? Good lad.' Groupie looked at his watch. 'Briefing's at Group at midday as usual. I'll send you a car with a pretty driver . . . and there's something else, Geoff.' He took an opened letter out of his pocket, and handed it over.

It carried the Air Ministry crest. It was all about the indignant British consul in Lisbon, and poor crazy Tommy Harrison. It finished:

Though it is medical opinion that the cat is a stress-engendered delusion, should the animal in question ever return to your airfield, she is to be painlessly destroyed, in accordance with govern-ment rabies quarantine regulations, and the body burnt immediately.

'Funny case,' said Groupie. 'But then she was a

212

strange cat.' And for the first time Geoff heard all about Lord Gort's flying.

Geoff almost said, 'She's my cat. She must've followed me here.'

But he was too full of a sick rage. She was *his* cat, not the RAF's to kill as it liked. After all she'd been through, all her faithfulness . . . to end like this.

'If she does turn up,' said Groupie, 'I'll get the RAF police to deal with her. Rotten job, but they're used to it.'

He didn't need to say any more. The RAF police were always dealing with unwanted animals, the pets of dead aircrew who'd bought them over Germany. They took them up to the firing-range and shot them through the head, and buried them there.

Tommy Harrison looked up from his bed in the funny-farm.

'She was with me,' he said, 'all the way. She turned up at the airfield for the flight home. Strolled around, rubbing against the legs of the Portuguese, who were helping to fuel the plane. When they turned their backs, she was aboard in a flash. Slunk in and burrowed down among the blankets on the rest-bed, just like she used to do on B-Baker. I saw her nip off when we landed at Hendon. She's on her way home, all right . . .'

He dropped his head again, and fumbled at the basket he was trying to weave, with trembling fingers.

'They call this occupational therapy,' he mumbled. 'It keeps you from thinking.'

Drops of water began to fall on the basketwork, from his hidden eyes.

213

22

Lord Gort was slow on her last journey, making her way north to Lincolnshire through the English spring. It was not that any sixth sense warned her of her approaching death, it was just that she was tired, with all the strangeness of travel, the odd smells of France and the even odder smells of Spain and Portugal, and the eternal need to *cope* with strangeness. The plane flight had been very dreadful. She could hear out of her right ear now, and the noise of the engines had been shattering.

And she was pregnant again. There had been at least one tom cat left in France, a huge, wild tabby with a scarred head, who had not vanished into a French rabbit pie.

She was always hungry, too. The grass and flowers might be growing, the trees bursting into blossom, but the young rabbits were still safe underground in their nests, and their parents well grown, wily and wary.

Heading north from London, she wandered up the wrong side of the Wash, and ended up staring out across the salt flats at New Hunstanton. Her person was there all right, on that faint blue line on the horizon. But she had learnt the hopelessness of trying to cross big water.

That same day, she nearly hanged herself; she was

leaping down inside a broken field shed when her collar caught round a nail.

She seemed to hang for ever, choking and kicking more and more feebly, with no one around her for miles to help.

And then the old collar snapped. She dropped to the ground, coughing and heaving for breath. Then she was sick, though she had very little to be sick with. Then she shook her head to clear it, and fled the evil spot. And as she fled, she felt something move inside her left ear.

Suddenly, she could hear perfectly.

Two weeks later, the farmer found the snapped collar and medal, read the medal with puzzlement, thought it was something to do with the Army and put it in his waistcoat pocket. Where months later, long after the end of Lord Gort's story, his wife found it and threw it away as rubbish.

A week later, still ravenous, Lord Gort got into a fight with a local tortoiseshell cat over the ancient, well-squashed body of a pheasant lying ground into the dust of the road. The fight was unusually savage. Lord Gort won in the end, at the price of a bleeding head and badly ripped ear. But the pheasant turned out to be nothing but feather and bone.

She was staggering with hunger when some children found her. If they'd been farm boys, it might have gone ill with her. But they were public school-girls, evacuees, with a sense of duty. They took Lord Gort to their teacher, who rang up the NSPCA.

The NSPCA in this case was Mrs Sample, the local vicar's wife, who kept six cats already. *Outside* cats, of course, who lived in the old vicarage stables because the vicar wouldn't have them in the house. So Lord Gort had her last litter in a stable as well. It didn't bother her; the stable was dry, the weather warm, the food now plentiful. The kittens prospered, and at eight weeks were found good homes very efficiently. With equal efficiency, Lord Gort was conveyed to the vet, neutered, and added to Mrs Sample's permanent collection.

Mrs Sample was her last great friend; Mrs Sample grew inordinately fond of her. Mrs Sample would come out every sunny evening to the stable and sit on a bale of straw and talk to the cats after they'd eaten. It was her one respite in a very busy day, full of good works.

She liked to give each of her strays a name; but she had a quirk. She would go to endless trouble to try to discover what the cats had been called before they'd strayed. She would call out every cat name under the sun to a new stray, to see if any made the cat prick its ears or twitch its tail. She was getting fairly desperate with this new one, who responded to *nothing*. She had run through all her repertoire; even descended to using male names, in case the previous owners had made a mistake about the sex, and called the cat 'Roger' or something in error.

And so she sat, trying out real oddballs like 'Egbert' or 'Timon' or 'Thucydides'. To no effect. Lord Gort sat on a bale of straw opposite, washing her whiskers after her meal. She didn't prick her ears or twitch her tail in the slightest.

The vicar came out to join his wife, sitting on the bale next to her. He was very fond of his wife, and not averse to cats, provided they stayed outdoors.

216

He smiled at her, a wry grin.

'Been listening to Lord Haw-Haw. He says there's going to be a heavy raid on Norwich tonight. Apparently we've looked our last on the beauties of Norwich cathedral. If you can *believe* him.'

'I wish you wouldn't listen to those German propaganda broadcasts,' said Mrs Sample absently, still watching Lord Gort. Why had the cat's ears suddenly *twitched*?

'Oh, old Haw-Haw's good for a laugh. Wouldn't miss him. Keeps me going.'

Again, as the vicar said 'Lord Haw-Haw' the cat's ears twitched.

'Surely they can't have called the poor cat Haw-Haw?' said Mrs Sample.

For a third time, the cat's ears twitched. The 'or-or' sound in 'Haw-Haw' was very like the 'or-or' sound in 'Lord Gort'.

'Haw-Haw,' called Mrs Sample. 'Haw-Haw, come to me!'

Obediently, the cat ran across and settled in her lap, purring.

'We *can't* call her Haw-Haw, poor thing. The children will throw stones at her. I shall call her "Hawkins" – that's a good English name – a hero's name. And it will fit on a medal for her new collar.'

And so 'Hawkins' it became. Lord Gort answered quite readily. She thought it meant 'food' anyway . . .

On the back of the medal went the vicar's phone number.

Lord Gort stayed a long and happy time with her last friend, though she often went north to look over the turbulent waters of the Wash towards

217

Lincolnshire. Having been neutered, and being well fed, she put on a last spurt of growth and became larger and plumper than she'd ever been.

She might have stayed there happily for ever. But one morning she sensed her person close, to the south-west; where there was dry land to run on.

And so she resumed her last journey.

23

Geoff did his new job somehow. He was bitterly unpopular at Group. He questioned doubtful gen too hard; he put the aircrew point of view too often; he made it all too real for his superiors; he made them feel guilty. He was not one of the boys.

But the aircrews loved him. He gave them the hard truth; he thought about their problems, understood how they felt. His bitter humour made them laugh at briefings and a laugh, however bitter, was always welcome.

There had been some muttering about his hand; how it got him out of the nasty job of flying bombers. When Geoff heard it, he flew two ops as an extra observer. That shut them up. Groupie told him never to do it again . . .

Fewer young men died in his wing than in other wings. But they still died. Sending them off to die with a laugh was near-unbearable to him. He knew too much. He knew the bomber-campaign wasn't working. He knew they were dying in vain.

The only relief was that, as June came on, the nights became shorter and shorter. Only five hours of real darkness. The bombers could not go far into Europe. Ops became less frequent. Fewer young men died.

He enjoyed the evenings when there was no op.

He'd knock off work early and help Florrie with the garden. Play outrageous bathtime games with Jeff, flooding the bathroom floor. Happy knowing his young men were out drinking in Louth or Lincoln, chatting up their popsies or shooting a line.

He sometimes thought about Lord Gort, glad she hadn't shown up. Glad there wasn't another innocent death on his conscience.

One evening, in late July, he was just closing up his office when Groupie walked in. Wearing ancient flying-gear. Looking like an enormous teddy-bear. Looking about fifteen years old.

'There's no raid tonight?' Geoff rose to his feet in alarm.

'No, no!' Groupie waved away any such unpleasant suggestion with a lordly hand. 'But I've wangled that Tiger Moth I promised you. *My* personal bloody aircraft. She's parked just outside. Let's go for a spin. C'mon, I've got you a helmet and goggles.'

Groupie in that mood was quite irresistible. They walked across the field to the little yellow biplane, looking as innocent as a dragonfly against the dark rows of bombers. It smelt good, too, just oil and petrol and fabric-dope, instead of shit and spew, carbolic and cordite, like the Wimpeys. A mechanic stood by, to swing the prop and pull aside the wheel-chocks.

'You want to take her, or shall I?' Groupie was struggling into the rear cockpit, like an egg trying to get into a too-small egg-cup. The Tiger Moth, a basic trainer, had controls in both cockpits.

'I'll take her,' said Geoff, hurriedly. God knew how

long it was since Groupie had flown a crate. And in his present boyish state . . .

Geoff switched on the ignition; gave the thumbs-up to the mechanic to swing her.

'Contact!' He revved the tiny buzzing engine, feeling its vibrations coming back through his hands, his backside. Suddenly, in spite of his missing fingers, he was nineteen again, just learning to fly, with all the glory of the clouds before him. As he took off, the Wimpeys dropped away below; like washing off filth in a shower.

He felt *clean*.

It came to an end quite suddenly, the loops and Immelmann turns, and the controlled spins through the dazzling sun-drenched canyons of the clouds, with Groupie behind him, babbling through the speaking-tube about Sopwith Pups and Hawker Furies and there never having been a monoplane built that could stunt like a biplane.

Twice the engine spluttered, then went dead, leaving only the sound of wind sighing through the wires.

'Christ,' said Groupie. 'We're clean out of gas. Two big boys like us, running out of gas. We'll never live it down.' He sounded not in the least repentant. 'Where the hell are we, Geoff?'

Geoff looked down through a cloud gap, at the blue shape of the Wash and the yellow bulge of East Anglia, running out to the pier at Cromer. Below them, a railway line and a city with a three-towered cathedral.

'Just south of Peterborough.'

'Plenty of airfields to choose from. Just don't prang her, for God's sake. She's my birthday present and Christmas all rolled into one . . .'

It was easy. The Tiger Moth was a sweet-tempered little thing, with engine or without. She sighed down as graceful as a glider, and Geoff made a perfect three-point landing on a bomber-field south of March.

Groupie knew the Groupie there. He called him 'Bunny' because in the last war he'd looked like a rabbit in his flying helmet. Bunny saw they were filled up with gas, and not a word to anybody. And they must stay for dinner in the mess; his group weren't flying that night, either. After dinner, the mess grew riotous. After putting in a call to Florrie, Geoff joined in a stupid and violent game involving five cushions, an old wheelchair and three soda-syphons. They rolled into bed at one in the morning, and didn't get up till ten. Then Bunny insisted they stay for lunch . . .

They finally took off after tea, with strict instructions to turn left at Norwich, and second right past the Howard Arms . . .

Far beneath them, Lord Gort was on her final journey again, round the south of the Wash.

24

It was late August when Lord Gort made it home to the little house on the northern edge of South Wedderby airfield. Across the garden, her person was asleep in his deckchair. Lord Gort was in no hurry, now she had him under her eye. She settled down contentedly in the heat of the August sun, among the dying wallflowers of the herbaceous border. She was very tired; her feet were cracked and sore. The humming of the insects was soothing. She almost slept herself; her eyes would droop, then shoot open again, to make sure her person was still there.

The first cool breeze of evening brought Geoff out of his doze, under the *Sunday Times* with its headlines about the Russian war going badly round Smolensk. He opened his eyes and said, 'Christ!'

Flo, sensitive to his every mood, stirred opposite him.

'Tea?' she said. 'Tea in the garden?'

'Do you see what I see?' he said, his face taking on that awful stillness it had when things were at their worst. She followed his eyes, and saw the black cat.

'Lord Gort?'

It suddenly felt cold in the garden. As if the sun had gone in, though it hadn't. They hurried across

223

to the cat, as to a road accident. The cat watched them, but did not stir her comfortable, furry heap.

'That's not Lord Gort,' said Flo. 'It's far too big and fat. It's *greasy*. And look at that mangled ear. It's been fighting – it's a *tom cat*.' She knew her voice was too shrill; she was so afraid of Geoff getting hurt again. She loved him, but despaired of understanding him. His sudden bursts of over-hilarity with young Jeff; his pits of black silence.

'There's a medal on the collar,' said Geoff. He made no move to touch it, so she reached down instead.

'There,' she said, her voice wild with relief. 'It's called "Hawkins". And there's a New Hunstanton phone number. I'll ring them, while I get the tea. They'll be worried about it.'

She hurried indoors, as if that would settle the matter. She was still dialling, when she saw Geoff return to his deckchair.

And the black cat follow him, and climb on his knee.

Just as Lord Gort used to do.

Saw him rub the cat under the chin, to make it raise its head,

Saw, even from a distance, the tuft of white hairs under the chin. Where Lord Gort used to have them . . .

By the time she got through to Mrs Sample, she was almost gabbling. And as she carried the tea-tray out, it was the turn of *her* hands to shake.

'It is called Hawkins,' she cried as she approached. 'Belongs to a lady called Sample – vicar's wife. She says we can keep her if we want – she's got six already.'

'It's Lord Gort,' said Geoff flatly. His face was very pale; his fingers almost *chewed* at the cat's fur with tension, making the cat flinch, and look about for a place to leap to. 'The white hairs are there, under her chin.'

'Lots of black cats have white under their chin,' she said, defensively.

'It's *Lord Gort*!' he blazed at her. 'And there's one way to prove it. I'm taking her across to B-Baker.'

'Is it still the same B-Baker?' Anything to save the cat's life; anything to stop Geoff hurting himself again, out of some black, misplaced sense of duty. Like he did so often . . .

'Same B-Baker. Different crew. Oldest crate on the base now.'

He got up, called to the cat, as he walked out through the gate.

'Have some tea first,' she called after him desperately. Anything to fend off disaster.

But he kept on walking; called to the cat again.

And gladly, with her tail up, she followed him to her certain death.

Geoff walked across the sunlit airstrip, his mind in a total confusion. The cat swished past him, brushing against his legs, as it had always done. And yet, *was* it her? She was too big, too muscular, less flirtatious, more middle-aged. He didn't want to be responsible for the death of an innocent cat called Hawkins . . .

The ground crew were working late on the port engine of B-Baker. They had the cowling off, and

225

were working stripped to the waist, brown backs gleaming in the setting sun. Geoff stopped ten yards back from where the access-hatch hung open. I'll give you a fair trial, puss, he thought. I won't hang you, unless you hang yourself . . .

Lord Gort hovered. Old familiar tempting smells came on the slight breeze that blew from the plane. The faint abiding smell of Tommy, still in the funny-farm. The faint abiding smells of Gregson and Tupper, Higgs and Smurthwaite, finished their tour of ops and gone to train young airmen. Only a cat could have smelt them, under the strong whiff of carbolic that the ground crew used to scrub out the plane after every op. Lord Gort took a curious step forward, The black hole of the access-hatch gaped invitingly, as all dark holes gape invitingly to a cat.

But she had unhappy memories of aircraft, too. The terrible torturing noise of that last flight. So she walked to the plane very hesitantly. Raised one paw to enter . . .

On the wing the ground-crew sergeant straightened up from the engine and called, 'Give her a try, Fenny.'

A hand waved through the side window of the cockpit.

The prop of the port engine jerked round; jerked round again, almost silently. Just the whirr of the electric starter-motor.

And then all the cylinders of the Bristol Pegasus roared into life.

The gale of hideous noise swept over Lord Gort.

She fled across the airfield like a black rocket, never to return.

Not guilty, thought Geoff. Or, at least, not proven.

'Not like old Lord Gort, sir, eh?' called the ground-crew sergeant. 'Got no taste for planes, that one.' He came across, wiping his hands on a piece of waste. 'Every black cat comes near the base, the lads think it's Lord Gort come back . . .'

'Are there many black cats?'

'There's a fat bugger hangs round the cookhouse. And C-Charlie's got one, but she won't fly. And the erks in the orderly room have got one, cos they think it's smart. Oh, you'd be amazed how many there are. But there'll never be another Lord Gort. Well, I mustn't stand talking here all night, sir. That won't buy the bairn a new shirt . . .'

Geoff walked back to the house thoughtfully.

That night, after the nine o'clock news, Geoff started arguing about his conscience again. With the cat on his knee.

'This cat never flew in a plane.'

'No, dear,' said Florrie, patiently.

'Noise of engines would've driven her mad.'

'Yes, dear.'

'She's far *bigger* than Lord Gort. You ought to feel the size of her bones.'

'Yes, dear.'

'And this ear.' His fingers played with the torn rag of flesh. 'And all black cats have a few white hairs somewhere.'

'Yes, dear.'

She watched them with a love so big it almost choked her; the man relaxed, the cat relaxed on his knee. That was how they used to sit, in the sane old days. Geoff almost looked his old self. *Almost.*

Geoff thought to himself, on the edge of sleep, the RAF has taken so many. Simpson and Shorty and Bill and Dan in the Blenheims. So many in the Wimpeys, he could no longer remember all the names. Here's one you don't get, RAF. This is one you can do without.

Lord Gort wriggled over on her back, careful not to fall off his knee. Idly, she swung a paw in the direction of his tie. In her small mind, all the places, all the people were fading. Even the memory of Mrs Sample was very dim. Her great days were over, her story was finished. All the rest of her life would be little strolls round a circular path of a few hundred yards; a little hunting, a lot of lying by the fire or in the sun. First here, where the black bombers flew in ever-increasing numbers; later in Beaminster, where nothing ever happened.

She was home with her person; she was warm, dry, full. That was all that mattered. She had become, again, a perfectly ordinary cat, not worth a second glance.

She gave a broken purr, and drifted off to sleep. Her whiskers twitched, her paws made little pouncing movements. In her dream, she was hunting mice.

Of what nationality is impossible to say.

Machine Gunners

'Some bright kid's got a gun and 2000 rounds
of live ammo. And that gun's no peashooter.
It'll go through a brick wall at a quarter of a mile.'

Chas McGill has the second-best collection of war
souvenirs in Garmouth, and he desperately wants
it to be the best. When he stumbles across the
remains of a German bomber crashed in the woods –
its shiny, black machine-gun still intact – he grabs
his chance. Soon he's masterminding his own war
effort with dangerous and unexpected results . . .

'Not just the best book so far written for
children about the Second World War, but also
a metaphor for now'
Aidan Chambers
Times Literary Supplement

Children of the Blitz

'We carried the cannon and machine-gun plus 300 rounds for the machine-gun and about 200 rounds in belt for the cannon, and laid them under the bushes well away from the crash. We went back after dark to collect our guns, transporting our loot home on Tony Cockerill's mother's bicycle.'
Boys aged fourteen and fifteen,
Withernsea, Humberside

Was there a secret Children's War from 1939–1945? Robert Westall believed there was when he wrote *The Machine Gunners*, a book about a gang of children who steal a machine-gun from a crashed German bomber. A few critics called it 'far-fetched'. But then the letters started rolling in . . . from people eager to tell the stories of their wartime exploits. These were indeed the Children of the Blitz.

'Many of those taking exams did far better than expected, since allowances were made for their having to dive under the desks several times during each exam.'
Boy aged sixteen, Sussex